MOLLY AND MRS. T

Susan Kay Gilmore

MOLLY AND MRS. T

Copyright © 2015 by Susan Kay Gilmore

Registered WGAw No. 1761265

Photographs by Avis Photography

ISBN 9780997567809
ISBN 10: 0997567805
Library of Congress Control Number: 2016907751
Gilmore's Write, Sunset Beach, CA

DEDICATION

It is my honor to dedicate this novel to my wise, loving Italian neighbor and friend, Lena Borgogna. At 100 years old, she's young beyond her years and is generously inspiring. May the world encounter many more loving souls like Lena.

ACKNOWLEDGEMENTS

One of the most rewarding experiences of writing this book was working with dedicated people who were supportive. They were all there when I needed them and remained engaged and committed throughout the entire project. This was my good fortune, and I thank each of them for their priceless contributions.

For my number one supporter, my husband, Bill
Beta Readers: Sandy Stevson, Georgia Mae Chidester,
Mike McGranahan, J. Raymond, and Bill Gilmore
Editor: Eve Gumpel
Photographer: Avis Rueweler of Avis Rueweler
Photography
Cover Models:
Mrs. 'T' - Gloria Suess, CEO, Mary's Kitchen, Orange, CA
Molly - Elizabeth Sprenkle

Elizabeth's Parents, Alma and Steve Sprenkle, who drove
her up from Chula Vista, CA, for the cover photo shoot—
just for the price of a tank of gas.
Technical advice and support: Victory Crayne, Author

C O N T E N T S

1

THE RIF AND TIFF

Molly Rae Armstrong stands at the apartment living room window and peers through the sheer curtains. A man with an angry expression is arguing intensely with a woman on the canal bank below. The poor woman appears to be crying--at least that's what her body language says. *He's probably a bully*, Molly thinks. Her eyes pan the landscape, and she sees a part of Brooklyn that's run down and decrepit--it reeks of decay and poverty.

A blue car pulls up and parks in front of the building. Molly tenses and rubs her light brown skin as though she has a chill. Her boyfriend, Jackson Wade, is home and Molly dreads his reaction to her news. How's she going to tell him that Jake laid her off at the café this morning? Revenues are down and she was the lowest in seniority and experience, so there was a Reduction in Force (RIF), and Molly had to go.

Jackson and Molly are both college students at Medgar Evers College, and the job paid her half of the rent and other expenses, like public transportation. She wrinkles her nose in frustration as she remembers she's got a paper due in a week and she'll have to search for a job, as well. She stopped at another café and a coffee shop on her way home today--to no avail. *What else can go wrong?* Molly laments.

Jackson's key turns in the lock and he comes in, laden with his backpack and laptop bag. He gives Molly a light kiss on her cheek and asks, "How's your day going, Sugar?"

Suddenly, Jackson seems so superficial--almost superfluous in her life. He appears to lack any true feelings of caring or consideration, and Molly isn't inspired. She's upset, but takes a deep breath and thinks she's about to find out how her day is really going.

Molly explains to Jackson how her former boss laid her off at the café this morning. Jake was kind to Molly when he laid her off--even sympathetic--but, of course, he had to do what's necessary to keep his business viable. Jackson's expression becomes unhappy.

"What are you going to do about it?" he blurts out abruptly.

Surprised by his abruptness, Molly gets a little defensive, which she regrets later. Jackson's a master at pushing buttons.

She offers, "I already stopped at two coffee shops on my way home. I'll update my resume tonight and keep looking, as much as my school schedule will allow."

Jackson inquires, "What's going to happen to school if you don't find work?"

Molly explains that the current semester is paid for--surely she'll have work before the next semester begins and can continue school. Almost angry, Jackson reminds Molly that the rent will be due in 2-½ weeks.

"I'm aware of that," Molly replies coolly, and guesses it's not a good time to discuss a contingency plan. She grabs her laptop, plops down on the couch and begins to work on her resume.

When dawn graces the horizon, Molly wakes up on the old, lumpy couch and sits up. Her back is stiff from the lack of support. The bedroom door is open, and Jackson has already left for school. Funny, she didn't feel a good-bye kiss or anything.

Molly mutters, "So, this is the way it's going to be." What did she expect, consolation and support? Regardless of Jackson, she's in survival mode now--he'll have to take a backseat. She's a junior in college, working on a BS in business administration, and she has too much at stake.

Molly doesn't have a class until 10:00 a.m., so if she gets her act together, perhaps she can hit a café or two on the way to school. She grabs a slice of peanut butter toast and some coffee to have while she straightens up the living room and arranges the contents of her backpack. Then she showers, gets dressed, and, as an afterthought, puts on some makeup. Her face is youthful and pretty, with wide brown eyes that are normally filled with joy. Today they're filled with concern. *Lip gloss,* Molly thinks, as she finds the tube and puts on the finishing touch.

As Molly exits the front door of the building, she stops to get her bearings. She's heard about a new coffee shop on Fern Avenue, so she heads in that direction. Walking in the sunshine and cool air, Molly begins to solidify her sense of purpose and determination. Her friends have told her that her middle name is *Persistence,* and she's determined to live up to it.

As she rounds the corner on Fern, she thinks the shop is about two blocks away. Sure enough, she spots the coffee shop across the street. It's got a great design with red bricks, racks full of pots planted with flowers and herbs, a wooden awning with shake shingles, and bricks painted blue with white clouds above the awning on the second story to the roof. There's a humorous hanging sign that says "BEAN TOO LONG CAFÉ - Gourmet Coffee, Tea, and Tasty Treats." A sign in the window states, "Dare to try our Raspberry-Chocolate Scones." Molly strolls by two bistro sets on the sidewalk and enters the front door.

There are only three customers in the café and two baristas in navy blue aprons. Molly approaches the counter and introduces herself to the barista who's close by. She notices how handsome he is, and he has a youthful face with hazel-colored eyes and smooth brown skin. He's tall, slender, and looks fit too.

The barista says, "I'm Donald Greene, the manager and proprietor. How may I help you, Molly?" She smiles and inquires about an opening for another barista.

Donald says, "I'm not sure. I'll have to ask Jasper."

"Who's Jasper?" Molly asks.

"The big boss," Donald replies. He looks toward the back room and says, "Jasper, can you come out here a minute?" Molly hears a rustling sound in the back room, and then through the curtain appears a Boston terrier with a bright-red collar.

Donald says, "This is Jasper, and he's a higher authority."

Molly reaches down to pet Jasper. "But, that still doesn't answer my question," she says as she straightens up. Jasper yelps when she stops petting him.

"Well, there's your answer," Donald says, motioning toward Jasper. "Unfortunately, he said 'not at this time.' We currently have three full-time baristas for weekdays and two part-time baristas for weekends and fill-in. One of the part-time positions may be open soon. Jasper would like a copy of your resume so he can follow-up with you."

Molly hands Donald her resume, and Jasper yelps again. "What's he saying this time?"

"He thanks you for stopping by, and he's offering you a free cup of our new java blend from Bali," Donald says with a warm smile.

"That sounds wonderful," Molly replies.

When Donald hands Molly her coffee, she thanks him and heads for the door. Then she stops, turns around, and with a slight nod of her head toward Jasper, she comments,

"Thank you for your kind consideration, Mr. Jasper. Next time I'll bring you some biscuits."

Donald smiles as Molly scoots off to school. He looks at Jasper and says, "Aye, she's a clever little wench, Master Jasper!" Jasper yelps in agreement. "Good," Donald says. "That's dog for aye!"

If Molly's late for English lit, Mr. Conrad may make a sarcastic remark in front of the class. She picks up her pace and begins to think about Donald Greene and Jasper. Besides having a warm smile, a great personality, and a cute dog, he's also got a sense of humor--and some fine looks. What a nice exchange they had--even though there isn't a job available. In spite of her current situation, she feels a sense of good spirits. *That was a gift*, she thinks, and smiles as she crosses the street to enter the school.

During the next two weeks, Molly visits three coffee shops, two cafes, two restaurants, and spends every other minute working on her junior year paper, Compelling Organizational Goals. This is a major project that has to be outstanding to set the stage for her senior year. She's concerned that she hasn't had a nibble on a job yet, and feels she needs to discuss alternatives with Jackson. The rent is due in three days, and she doesn't have enough money to pay her half. She's still sleeping on the couch and hasn't seen much of Jackson in the last two weeks--he's being very reserved. With her usual flair for the dramatic, Molly thinks, *the dénouement has yet to unfold!* And, it sure does.

Jackson lets himself in, puts down his things and gives Molly a chilly "Hi!"

There's no time like the present, Molly thinks. "Jackson, I need to talk with you about the rent situation."

Jackson asks, "Have you got your half of the rent together?"

"Not yet! It would totally wipe out my savings, and I wouldn't have any money for other expenses."

"Well, I don't want to find a third person to live here--this place is too small. What about work?" Jackson challenges.

"I've applied at eleven places and haven't had a response--the purse strings are really tight right now." Molly continues, "May I owe you $50 on the rent while I continue to look for a job?"

Getting testy, Jackson sarcastically responds with, "Well, I can't afford to take on some charity case."

Hearing this, Molly snaps and blurts out, "Just the qualities I've always wanted in a man--no respect and no compassion." She grabs her rolling carry-on bag and starts to pack.

Molly adds, "Don't worry; I won't be an imposition any longer." She puts on her coat, zips her bag, grabs her backpack, and heads for the door.

Jackson inquires, "Where are you going?"

Molly doesn't even bother to look back and retorts, "What do you care, Jerk?" The door slams shut and she's gone--where, she doesn't know--but she's gone. Big, hot tears start to run down her face.

2

RUDY THE SAGE

Molly is really angry with the male gender now, and mumbles through her tears, "What a bunch of self-serving, disrespectful, thoughtless, sexist slobs." She walks toward the canal, pulling her bags behind her. On a whim, she decides to look for the guy who made that woman cry. Even though it's totally irrational, she's on a roll and takes a right onto the canal bank. The bank is covered with gravel, so she has to pick up her bags and carry them.

There's a lot of brush--mostly dead--along the side of the canal. Molly walks slowly and inspects the bushes. Finally she sees a camouflage-covered tent, and asks aloud if anyone's there. She thinks she hears someone stir, so she persists. It takes some coaxing, but Molly continues, "I can hear you stirring around in there." After a few seconds of silence, a man's face appears in the opening. He looks to be around 45, has a crop of long black hair pulled back in a ponytail, studs in his ears, tattoos on his lower arms, steel-gray eyes, and a weathered face. Molly thinks, *Don't trust your instincts any longer, girl!* She asks the man if she can speak with him for a minute.

"What for?" he asks with an undeniable British accent.

"This isn't a social visit, Limey. I won't take much of your time," Molly states. He cautiously gets out of his tent and climbs onto the canal bank.

"I'm Rudy Lee," the man says, "and whom am I speaking with?"

She doesn't soften. "I'm Molly."

Rudy asks, "How might I help you, Molly?"

Immediately she launches into her story of having lived in the apartments across the street, and seeing him with a woman he appeared to be scolding. "She looked like she was sobbing, and I just wanted to meet the heartless man who would do such a thing." Before he can respond, Molly blurts out, "Why did you have to be so mean to her?"

Rudy gazes off into space and remains quiet for a few seconds. Then he turns to face Molly and inquires, "And, what makes this any of your business?"

"I'm also a woman who has been scorned, and I believe it was despicable behavior," says Molly, as tears well up in her eyes.

Rudy can see that Molly is out of sorts, so he remains cool. His facial expression changes to sadness and he volunteers, "That woman is my sister, Allison Lee. I felt bad that I kind of lost it, but I scolded her out of love."

Molly asks incredulously, "Love?"

Rudy looks Molly in the eyes and says, "Yes, she's using again and I'm really afraid it won't be long before the drugs kill her." Molly softens, feeling sorry that she invaded Rudy's privacy. *What am I doing?*, she thinks.

One skill that Rudy Lee does have is his ability to read people. Molly's heartbreak is obvious, but Rudy senses there's a lot more to her story--almost a hopeless thread. He believes the best way to help Molly at this time is to confide in her.

"Alli and I only have each other. She's been through four treatment programs but always relapses. I can't imagine what the next step will be, or what will happen to Alli," Rudy laments.

"I'm so sorry that this is happening to you and Alli, and embarrassed that I challenged you so harshly," Molly replies.

"Oh, no," Rudy says. "Sometimes we forget about another person's perspective. To you, it would appear that I was being abusive and mean to Alli."

Molly starts to shake a little bit when a cool breeze comes up. "Are you all right?" Rudy inquires.

"I haven't eaten much today, and I'm getting a little light-headed," Molly responds. "I just became homeless and I need to find a shelter. Do you know where a women's shelter is?"

Rudy guides Molly to sit on her carry-on bag while he gives her directions to the Alma de Lucy shelter, which is about fifteen blocks away.

"It's almost sundown; do you want me to walk with you?" Rudy asks. Molly declines and thanks Rudy for his kind gesture. She believes that if she leaves right now, she'll be there before dark and in time for supper.

Rudy's face shows concern, and he becomes insistent. "Molly, you've got to get to the shelter before dark." He explains to Molly that she'll have to walk through the *Outer Side* to get to Lucy's, and it's an extremely dangerous area.

"The *Outer Side* is like a third-world slum--you'll see, hear, and smell everything. Even if you cover your nose and mouth or hold your breath, the stench will remain with you for a long time," Rudy tells Molly.

"I'm concerned about your safety, especially since you're upset and vulnerable," Rudy continues, "and I'd feel better if you'd allow me to walk with you."

Molly's touched by Rudy's brotherly concern and shows her sense of humor when she replies, "Aye, Master Robin of Locksley!"

Rudy lets out a hearty laugh and is pleased with Molly's response. He picks up her cases and says, "C'mon, matey, we'll walk and talk."

Rudy becomes serious after they establish a brisk pace. "Now, Molly, pay close attention to these pointers--they'll help you survive." Molly acknowledges Rudy, and he continues.

"Whatever you do, always be aware of your surroundings, and be prepared to react. Use your peripheral vision instead of making eye contact, especially if they try to talk with you. You'll eventually figure out whom you can trust. And, from now on, I'd carry your bags instead of dragging them, or they might not be yours very long. When you walk, keep your back straight and shoulders back like you're brimming with self-confidence and ready to take on the world."

Rudy cautions, "They may be less likely to try to victimize you. There's no such thing as civil liberties in the *Outer Side*, and no policemen or paramedics will respond. More than any other time in your life--you're on your own." Molly takes Rudy's arm and tries not to look terrified.

There aren't words to describe what Molly and Rudy witness on the way to Alma de Lucy. Some scenes touch Molly and tug at her heartstrings. A mother is breast feeding her infant, and they look like Holocaust survivors--skin and bones with sunken eyes and deep, dark circles under them. She sees poor, elderly people with urine-stained clothes, confused and muttering unintelligibly, and obviously lacking health and dental care. She spies children going through people's belongings while their victims are passed out or sleeping--possibly dead. A man beats up a woman who could be a prostitute and illicit sex and drug deals are going down everywhere. It is just block after block of cardboard boxes, tents, sleeping bags, and people lying on the sidewalk without any protection. Everywhere Molly looks, she sees abject poverty, grief, emotionless faces, anger, hatred, crime, begging, sobbing, hunger, illness, and pain--every affliction imaginable. The suffering is unbelievable, and so is the noxious stench. Molly's nostrils burn when she inhales the pungent air--it feels like she's breathing an acid composed of urine, feces, vomit, and rotting food. Molly starts to cough, and she quickens her step. She becomes quiet for some time and Rudy knows the emotional turmoil she's experiencing.

"Two more blocks," he says. "Hang in there!"

"I feel so vulnerable and afraid, Rudy," Molly states earnestly.

"Fear is a natural reaction to this environment, Molly. And if you become reactionary, you'll become vulnerable."

"So, what are you trying to tell me?" she responds. "Don't react?"

"Correct--when it's appropriate not to react. You seem to have good instincts. You'll know," Rudy replies.

They walk the last two blocks in silence, and Rudy motions for Molly to turn left into a dark alley between two buildings. At the end of the buildings they make another left turn and on their right is a gray building with a light and a small, unpretentious sign that reads 'Alma de Lucy.'

Molly can see light through the windows, but can't see anything else because the windows are too high. She motions to the sign and asks Rudy what Alma de Lucy means.

"It means *Soul of Lucy*, or *Lucy's Soul*," Rudy replies. "Once you get to know her, you'll discover that she has a lot of soul."

Molly thanks Rudy for his kind words and invaluable assistance. Rudy tells her he'll check with her in a few days to see how she's settling in. And he reminds her that he hasn't heard her story yet.

He smiles at Molly and extends his hand to shake hers. "When I become afraid and apprehensive, I tell myself that 'Fear' is bravery turned inside out. That's what we need to do, Miss Molly—think of fear as bravery and proceed with confidence. We can help each other too. If you could use a friend and you're willing, I'm willing," he says with a smile. "And, I'm certain that God is on our side."

Molly grabs Rudy's hand and shakes it warmly, turns around, takes a deep breath, and rings the doorbell at Alma de Lucy. She glances over her shoulder, but there's no sign of Rudy--it's like he evaporated. "I'm on my own now," Molly says to herself.

3

ALMA DE LUCY

Weariness has set in; Molly wants something to eat and a space to sleep. She vows to develop a survival plan tomorrow and worries about getting to school on time.

A woman's voice is heard through a speaker on the wall by the door. "Who's there, and what's your purpose?" she inquires.

"My name is Molly Armstrong, and Rudy Lee brought me here because I need shelter," Molly replies.

The woman narrowly opens the door to view Molly. Swallowing her last bite of supper, she opens the door and says, "I'm Lucy Mercado, the shelter proprietor. Come on in so we can talk about your situation, Dear. Have you had supper?"

"No, ma'am," Molly responds, as she steps into a dimly lit hallway.

Lucy looks at her and says, "I believe there's enough food left from supper for me to put together a plate for you. Come this way!"

To her right, at the end of the hall, Molly can see light and hear women's voices talking softly. Lucy turns left and Molly follows her into an empty dining room with four long tables in two rows and folding chairs on both sides. Lucy is an attractive, middle-aged Hispanic woman, wearing jeans, sandals, and a bright-colored tunic. She has beautiful skin, shiny, long black hair--clipped on top of her head-- and kind brown eyes, reflecting wisdom beyond her years.

"So, my Brit friend brought you here?" Lucy inquires.

"Yes. I'd never been through the *Outer Side* before, so Rudy insisted on escorting me here. I'm glad he did," Molly wearily replies.

Lucy responds, "Rudy can be a little rough around the edges at times, but he's really a good person at heart."

She pulls some papers out of a file folder and hands them to Molly. "Here's an application for you to complete, the Alma de Lucy Ground Rules--which we'll review together if you qualify--and a list of local soup kitchens and food banks, since we don't serve lunch here. You can start to fill these out while I get your supper."

"Thank you," Molly says as she gets out her pen.

Alma de Lucy Shelter Ground Rules

Guests must be in the building by 10 p.m. every night, including weekends. The door is locked at 10 p.m. and is not unlocked until 8 a.m. the following morning. The only exceptions are employment or school with legitimate documentation.

Guests cannot be in the shelter between 10 a.m. and 2 p.m. The only exceptions are for the disabled, sick, or a high-risk pregnancy, and medical documentation is required. The rule will not apply when the outside temperature is 36 degrees or below.

The television in the living room will be turned off at 10 p.m. daily.

Guests may have electronic devices, including radios, with ear buds or headsets only. They may also have cell phones, but they will be silenced during all meals and at 10 p.m.

No smoking of any substance.

No drinking of alcohol or any illegal liquid.

No fighting or loud arguments.

All guests must sign in and out on the clip-board beside the front door when arriving or departing.

Lucy Mercado, Manager

Resident Name: _____

Date: _____

Of course, the application requires the name and number of a contact, and Molly doesn't know whom to put down. There's no way she'll put *Jackson the Jerk* on there. Her father left the family when Molly was six years old, her mother died when she was seventeen, and her only sibling, a brother named Jason, was placed in a foster home because he was only seven. Molly was self-sufficient, so she stayed with her grandmother, who wasn't very mobile, capable, or interested in caring for small children. When Molly was eighteen, she went to apply for custody of Jason, but he had fallen through the cracks and Child Protective Services (CPS) couldn't locate him. Perhaps he ran away. That was six years ago; Jason would be thirteen now, but Molly will never give up on finding him. She sighs and puts the Medgar Evers Business Administration Department secretary's name and phone number as a contact on the application. Lucy brings in a plate of food for Molly, which she devours.

Lucy sits down and begins to review Molly's application. "What relation is your contact Donna Scott to you?" she inquires.

"She's a friend," Molly responds. "I don't have any family here."

Lucy isn't fooled by Molly's answer and says, "I understand."

There's a slight pause before Lucy asks her next question, "Have you had a chance to read the Ground Rules?"

"Yes, and I have a question about the curfew." After Lucy nods, Molly explains that she's a full-time student at Medgar Evers and just lost her job and her lodging. If Wi-Fi isn't available at the shelter, Molly will have to do all of her computer work at the college library, which closes at 10:00 p.m. Lucy advises Molly that she'll probably have to leave the library by 9:30 p.m. to make curfew. She also gives Molly information about applying for unemployment benefits, noting that jobs are hard to find due to too many government regulations and not enough educational programs for potential applicants.

"It's like they don't want anyone to succeed," Lucy says under her breath.

At this point, the shelter has grown quiet. "There's one more thing I need to tell you about staying here," Lucy volunteers. "All guests have routine chores to do, which I assign weekly. I don't have any other help. Give me a copy of your class schedule, and I'll try to work around it."

Molly smiles and says, "You mean I can stay here?" Lucy confirms that Molly can stay, but advises her that it's just for thirty days. She gives her a security code for the keypad by the front door and cautions her that it's turned off at exactly 10:00 p.m.

"Also, all twenty cots are filled right now, so you'll have to sleep on the floor until a bed is available," Lucy states. "It's getting late; I'll give you a quick tour, and then you can get settled." They stand up, and Molly looks up at a big clock on the dining room wall. For the first time today, she feels relieved and hopeful.

Off the dining room is an alcove with two washers, dryers, and vending machines filled with laundry products. There's also a door that leads outside to a small patio. Lucy motions to the patio and says, "This is where our guests go to smoke cigarettes." She doesn't say anything else, but wrinkles up her nose somewhat.

Lucy then takes Molly into the living room where there are two couches, a few chairs, and a TV. Two small windows, very high up, can only be opened and closed with a long pole with a hook on the end. Molly knows this is for security purposes. Lucy's living quarters are off the living room, and she has a small bedroom and bathroom between her room and the shelter's kitchen. All guests at Alma de Lucy know that they can't dally in the bathroom. Lucy's bathroom is available to guests only for emergencies, such as vomiting and diarrhea, when the other bathroom is occupied. The guests' bathroom is off the sleeping room and has two toilets and showers. Unfortunately, showers need to be scheduled and can't last longer than ten minutes. *Whew, so many rules,* Molly thinks.

Before going to the sleeping room, Molly steps back into the dining room for a minute. Lucy asks, "Is there something else, Molly?" Molly asks Lucy about the guests who stay there, as she wants to get along with them and feel comfortable.

"I won't sugarcoat anything," Lucy responds. "These are very vulnerable, mostly transient people--two-thirds of whom have mental illness or substance abuse problems."

Lucy sighs and continues, "In the old days the mentally ill were hospitalized, but this isn't economically feasible today. Now, institutions bring them to the *Outer Side* and dump them on the streets."

"Isn't that dangerous?" Molly asks.

"Of course it is!" Lucy replies. "Most of them are too confused to take their medications, so they can have aggressive or violent behaviors. It's horribly sad, but if you ask any of them where home is, most will say that the *Outer Side* is their home. And, for most disenfranchised souls, it offers refuge where they can be free and, hopefully, become well and whole," she adds.

Molly gets a glimmer of Lucy's compassionate side and notes, "That's what the human spirit strives for. I'll help when I can, Lucy."

Lucy taps Molly's shoulder and says, "Come on, Molly. I'll show you where the bathroom is and your little corner of the world. There should be a cot available in five to six days." Lucy pulls a blanket, pillow, and bottle of water out of a hall closet, hands them to Molly, and they head toward the sleeping room.

The sleeping room is dark and fairly quiet now--Molly hears someone snoring softly. Twenty small cots are lined up and down both sides of the room, with about twelve inches between them. Molly thinks about how close the cots are, but if they can get more women in here and help them, it's understandable. The front of the room has more space, as the bathroom door is to the left. In the center of the wall is a small table with a night-light and some books, with wall mirrors on each side.

Lucy motions Molly to the corner of the room on the right side and whispers, "This is the only space we have available, Molly. Sorry!"

Molly whispers back to Lucy, "I'm grateful for any space you have. Goodnight, Lucy, and thank you!"

Lucy leaves as Molly takes her pajamas out of her bag. She then puts her bags in the corner--like a head-board--and folds the blanket into fourths on the floor. After Molly goes in the bathroom and gets ready for bed, she lies down with her pillow, and uses her coat as a cover. Tears form in Molly's eyes, and she tries to suppress them. This has been one of the most intense days of her life, and she's overwhelmed. She tries to review the unbeliev-able events of the day, but like a savior, weariness swoops in to envelop and embrace her like a cool fog. There's a brief tug of war in which sleep is winning, and it seems to be saying, "You've had food, and so I'm what you need the most now. You can worry about more food and Wi-Fi tomorrow!" Molly's eyes close and her respirations slow as she surrenders--for now, sleep will solve everything.

4

GLAD TO BE 'GLAD'

Somehow Molly manages to sleep deeply on that hard floor, but she's stiff when she wakes up. *I seem to have more stiffness than joints and muscles to put it in*, Molly thinks. The first thing she does is put her name on the shower list, and then she introduces herself to the other guests. Some of the women are withdrawn, but a few appear to be somewhat outgoing--it's a real mixed bag. A woman named Jackie is friendly, and from the look of things, about eight months pregnant. Molly wonders how it will be handled when Jackie goes into labor--if that happens within her thirty days at the shelter. *Maybe there's a rule or a clipboard to sign*, she muses. A little smile crosses her face when she realizes she hasn't lost her sense of humor.

One of the rules Molly appreciates most is that eating breakfast in your pajamas or nightgown is allowed, although many of the guests sleep in their clothes. She goes to the dining room to eat in her PJs while waiting for her shower. The kitchen has a Dutch door, so guests choose from a simple menu on the bulletin board, order at the door, and wait a couple of minutes while Lucy and her helper put it together. Breakfast pretty much consists of cold cereal, instant oatmeal, scrambled eggs, toast and fruit. Jackie told her that sometimes they get sausage with their eggs on Sunday, if they're lucky. Molly pours herself a cup of coffee while she waits for her breakfast. She wonders if they ever have toasted bagels and cream cheese. Her mind starts to wander to her leisurely mornings at the apartment with the coffee machine and all of the tasty, flavored coffees. She's snapped back to reality when Lucy hands her breakfast tray to her at the kitchen door. Lucy is very busy cooking eggs, but stops long enough to say, "Good morning, Molly. Did you sleep well?"

"Morning, Lucy. Yes, I slept better that I thought I would. I guess I was really tired." Molly sits down to eat and joins in some idle chitchat with a couple of the women.

When it's Molly's turn to shower, she discovers that she needs the skills of a time-management wizard to brush her teeth, shower, wash her hair and shave her legs in ten minutes. "Now I know what warp speed feels like, and there isn't any time left for makeup," she says to herself. It dawns on her that the two mirrors on the sleeping room wall must be for fixing hair and putting on makeup--for the ladies who are so inclined. She dresses quickly and throws on a little makeup. There's a coffee shop on the way to school where she wants to inquire about a job. Molly grabs her coat and bags and remembers to sign herself out on the clipboard by the front door. The day is sunny when she steps outside. With resolve--and trying to be positive--Molly says, "It's just a matter of time until I have the shelter routine mastered. This is my life for now, and I'll make it work." She takes a big breath and leaves.

Of course the coffee shop doesn't have any openings at this time, and Molly is getting so tired of hearing that phrase. Her pace quickens when she checks the time on her cell phone. She decides to experiment with the route to school--not necessarily the shortest route, but the safest one. If she sees Rudy, he can help her with this, but for now she'll pray for good judgment and do the best she can. Molly's last class ends at 1:00 p.m., and she'll head straight for the library. Hopefully, she can finish her studies in time to navigate through the *Outer Side* and get back to the shelter before dark. Reading assignments can be done at the shelter, and she can create documents on her laptop computer--as long as she doesn't need the Internet. *'I'll make it work'* will become my new motto, Molly thinks as she arrives on campus.

The unknown can be so unsettling. Molly's distracted in class and is clearly having problems focusing on her studies. After her last class, she goes straight to the library.

Most of her assignments are reading, so she won't have to stay long--just long enough to check her e-mails, social media sites, and do a little research. She sees Jennifer Woods from her English lit class studying at a table and decides to sit close to her. Molly feels a little insecure at this time and wants to feel a connection with someone she's familiar with. Walking over to the table, she thinks of one thing she's grateful for and whispers, "Thank heavens for free Wi-Fi!"

Molly manages to finish her computer work in forty-five minutes, says goodbye to Jennifer, and takes off. The street she decides to walk down has some homeless residents on the sidewalk in tents and cardboard boxes.

Two adolescent boys are walking along and stop when they see Molly coming. One assumes a casual stance, hooks his thumbs in his pockets, and says, "Look at this hot little chicky!" The other boy shakes his hand and makes a sizzling sound. Molly ignores their verbal advances and tries to get out of their path, but accidentally kicks a foot that's sticking out of a large cardboard box.

A shrill voice cries, "Ouch! What are you trying to do?" The two boys take off.

An elderly white woman peers out of the hole in the box, and Molly apologizes. "I'm very sorry, lady. I was trying to avoid those stupid boys, and I didn't see your foot."

The woman struggles to get to her feet, and Molly helps her.

"Are you hurt?" Molly asks as the woman stands and takes a few steps.

"I appear to be fine, Child," she replies and turns to face Molly. She's just a little wisp of a thing with beautiful, long gray hair, and twinkly blue eyes—*just like Mrs. Santa Claus*, Molly thinks. Her back is slightly humped and the joints in her hands are gnarly, but other than that, she appears to be aging gracefully--in spite of the hardships of homelessness.

"What's your name, Child?" the woman inquires.

"I'm Molly Armstrong," she answers, "and who are you?"

"I'm Gladys Mae Teaberry," the lady says with a faint southern drawl and a proud smile, "but you can call me Glad."

"Glad?" Molly inquires.

"Yes, Child, *Glad to live another day*." The two women chuckle and shake hands. An orange tabby cat strolls regally out of the cardboard box and stretches.

"There was a cat in your box," Molly says.

"Oh, that's my soul mate, Axel," Glad replies. Molly says hello to Axel and reaches down to pet him.

Glad says, "You must be special, Child. He hardly ever lets strangers pet him."

Molly smiles. "I just love big, orange boys," she says as she scratches him under the chin.

She straightens up. "I have to go now, Glad, but may I check on you tomorrow?"

"Sure, Molly, maybe we can visit more then," Glad replies. They shake hands again and Molly leaves for the shelter.

The next street may be a good route to cut over to the shelter, but when Molly gets there, it's not a street, it's a deserted alley. Her better judgment says not to use the alley, but right in the entrance to the alley is a dumpster with some carpet tiles in it. Molly inspects the tiles and they're clean, so she takes six of them. *These will add some softness to that shelter floor,* she thinks. As she starts to leave, she giggles and says to herself, "Wow! I just made my very first dumpster dive."

Walking actually feels good, and it gives her an opportunity to review her day and make some mental footnotes. The shrill ring of her cell phone splits the air and startles Molly. It's been a while since she got a call. The phone display says *J. Wade,* and Molly hits the END button. *There's no way I want to talk with Jackson,* she thinks. *And I hope he has a guilty conscience for the way he treated me.*

Molly's phone rings again, and she starts to reach for the END button, but the display says *Don Green.* This time Molly answers with a smile. Donald is following up to advise her that the part-time barista position hasn't opened up yet. He explains that the barista is a single mother who either needs to find full-time work or something to augment her hours while continuing to work at Bean Too Long. Molly appreciates the information; then she inquires about *President* Jasper, which pleases Donald.

"I'm glad you asked," he responds, "because Jasper has requested that we take you out to dinner. He has some questions about your resume."

Molly tries desperately to hedge--the last thing she wants Donald to know about her is that she's homeless. It's humiliating, and she just can't date at a time like this. Donald persists and is very persuasive, but Molly only agrees to stop by the shop later for a drink.

He replies, "I look forward to seeing you again. We'll talk about dinner when you get here."

They say goodbye and Molly experiences some fluttering in her chest, which she tries very hard to suppress and ignore. *Darn those butterflies*, she finally thinks. Molly walks the rest of the way to the shelter in a more lighthearted mood. She anticipates long, hard days in her life at this time, but at least she's unencumbered by an arrogant, egotistical, thoughtless boyfriend. Actually, she decides, surviving on her own is giving her a real sense of empowerment and strength. "A new day is dawning!" Molly whispers to herself, and smiles.

There's just enough time to take the carpet tiles to the shelter and freshen up. On her way out the door, she tells Lucy that she won't be there for dinner. Molly has some time to think en route to the coffee shop. She's nervous and feels she shouldn't start dating now--her life is complex enough. *However*, she argues in her mind, *I'm going to*

need some good friends to help me get through all of this. She realizes that could just be a rationalization, but she'll shoot for friendship with Donald. At least she's made a decision.

Molly walks about eight blocks to Bean Too Long. As she approaches, she can see Donald through the window, cleaning tables and singing.

The coffee shop is empty when Molly walks in, and she asks, "Is that why you don't have any customers?"

He smiles and asks "Why?"

Molly replies, "You started singing, and they all left."

"Ouch," Donald says, feigning a hurt look. Molly grins, as *President* Jasper yelps and appears from the back room. She kneels down, and Jasper runs to her.

"Watch out, Molly, he loves the ladies," Donald warns.

Molly says to Jasper, "Oh, fickle, are you?" and begins to play with him.

"And what would be your pleasure, Miss?" Donald asks.

"A skinny decaf latte sounds good," Molly responds. Donald fixes a couple of lattes and a sandwich for Molly, and since the weather is nice and the shop is empty, they go outside to sit at a bistro table.

He puts everything on the table and says to Molly, "I took the liberty of fixing you a chicken, tomato, lettuce, and Gouda cheese sandwich on multigrain bread."

She looks up at Donald and replies, "Wow! That looks good; thanks, Donald." She hasn't said she's hungry, but the truth is, she's starving.

Donald sits down. "That's a little formal--please call me Don." Molly smiles and notes how kind and attentive he is.

Suddenly, the peaceful evening is shattered by a loud, angry crowd pouring out of a building across the street. People spill out onto the sidewalk and are riled up about something--their voices are getting more animated and loud. Don gets concerned and suggests they move back inside.

As they pick things up and move, Molly asks, "What's that all about?"

Don states, "I think it has something to do with alleged police brutality. They've been gathering all day."

In an attempt to learn more about Molly, Don asks, "Where do you stand on mobs?"

With an inquisitive look on her face, she asks "Flash mobs?"

Don grins and says, "No, like the angry mob across the street."

Molly sighs and responds, "In my young life, I've discovered and believe that it depends on whom you talk to."

With interest, Don leans forward and replies, "If you talk with enough people, you're bound to meet someone with the same point of view as your own."

"Exactly," Molly responds. "And what you do at that point is critical. You can start to form a group of fans, or supporters for the cause, or . . ."

Don interjects, ". . . or you can become a group of activists, anarchists, or, worse yet, terrorists--whatever it takes to facilitate the cause." Don and Molly continue their deep conversation, moving on from mobs and terrorism to a thorough discussion of their educational goals. Don and

Molly are both business majors, as he's in the economics and business master's program at the City College of New York.

"I go to night school three nights a week, and only have twelve credits left--plus I'm looking for an internship to complete," Don says.

"Wow! That's a challenging schedule--in addition to your duties here. I'll bet *President* Jasper gets lonely," Molly replies.

"Jasper's fine. A neighbor takes him out mid-evening for a little jaunt."

Molly smiles and says, "Gee, I'm lucky that you and Jasper make time for me."

Don returns the smile. "Well, you're our favorite customer!"

"This is my favorite coffee shop," Molly coyly replies, "and you seem to be here 24/7."

"Oh, no. Ben works the p.m. shift, but I'm covering a couple of his hours while he takes care of something important."

Around 6:30 p.m., Molly advises Don that she has to go home to do her homework. If she leaves at this time, she should have enough light to get back to the shelter safely. Don inquires if he may take Molly home, and she declines. She writes her e-mail address on a placemat, hands it to Don, invites him to call her again, and asks how much she owes for the tasty food and drink.

Don answers, "Those are compliments of the house-- the *President* insists!"

Molly giggles and thanks them both. She and Don then acknowledge that they enjoyed the conversation; he opens the door for her and touches her hand before she leaves.

"Which role is it, then," he asks, "supporter or anarchist?"

With a laugh, Molly replies, "Ha, I can't even support myself right now. See you, Don and Jasper!" She flashes a big smile as she turns to leave. Molly's level head, intelligence, honesty, and sense of humor impress Don--not to mention the fact that she's really cute. Also, they seem to be on similar planes, which he feels is positive. The next thing Don hears is a yelp from Jasper.

"Do you like her, boy?" Don inquires. Jasper yelps again, and Don replies, "So do I."

5

GLAD TO BE MRS. 'T'

Molly doesn't have a class until 10:00 a.m., so she decides to start the day early and visit Rudy. He can give her advice about the routes to take through the *Outer Side*. She hates to go back to her old neighborhood and hopes she doesn't run into Jackson. When she gets to the canal bank she doesn't see any activity across the street, and she spies Rudy walking toward the sidewalk with a woman.

He sees Molly and says, "Hey, Molly! I'm glad to see you. I want you to meet my sister, Allison."

Molly extends her hand. "Molly Armstrong; glad to meet you, Allison."

Alli shakes Molly's hand. "Allison Lee, but you may call me Alli." She's a petite, striking, thirtyish woman with long, straight black hair, bangs, and beautiful green eyes. Molly thinks, *Wow! It's true what they say about the Brits beautiful skin--Alli's skin is amazing--in spite of the dark circles under her eyes*. Alli is somewhat disheveled, but is lucid and tries to smile. Her eyes betray her, however, as they reflect anxiety and hopelessness. Silently, Molly prays that someone can reach out and help Alli before it's too late--she would like to know the Alli who's hidden beneath this cloak of darkness and despair.

Alli says, "Sorry, but I've got to go to an appointment." She kisses Rudy on the cheek and takes off.

When Molly turns to Rudy, his face is still full of compassion and love for his sister. He meets her gaze and says, "Pray for her, Molly. She's in group therapy again." Molly touches his sleeve and assures him that she will.

Rudy shifts the focus. "I want to hear all about what's happening in your life, Molly. Do you have time for tea?"

"I have about an hour," Molly replies. Rudy smiles, picks up her bags and they walk to his tent. He motions her to a folding chair outside the tent, pours some bottled water into a beat- up pot, and puts it on a fire.

"It's hardly the Ritz, Honey, but we'll make do," he says, as he rummages around in a cardboard box for two cups. Then he brings out a beautiful British tin with teabags in it. Molly raises her eyebrows, impressed.

"In spite of my circumstances, some things--like tea-- are still sacred," Rudy states, and Molly gives him a smile.

Rudy is delighted that Molly sought him out for advice to help her navigate around the *Outer Side*, and he writes down a lot of tips for her. She tells him about school, how she's settling in at the shelter, and how nice Lucy is. Molly agonizes about what she'll do at the end of thirty days, however, as she hasn't found a job and doesn't know what to do.

Rudy says, "Don't give up, Molly--you're intelligent and resourceful."

She looks down at the ground and says, "I've thought about dropping out of school."

"Don't do that," Rudy responds quickly. "You only have a year left in school. And, although the new road you're traveling down looks ominous and scary, keep your eyes looking forward and paddle like hell." Rudy smiles.

"Sound advice," Molly says, looking a little doubtful. "In other words, don't look back. You're starting to sound a little bit like Winston Churchill." She stands up to leave.

Rudy's look becomes cherubic. "Oh, you're going to become a fine sparring partner. Before you go, isn't there something else you want to tell me about?" Rudy inquires.

"What do you mean?" Molly asks.

"Well, call it intuition, but I believe that something positive is happening in your life--I feel it," he says with an inquisitive grin.

"There's a very tentative situation, but it will have to wait until our next visit," Molly says as she picks up her bags. Rudy takes them from her and says he'll walk her to the street. Molly thanks him for the tea and thinks, *Man, these Brits are psychic, too.*

After school, Molly clips along with her bag to go check on Glad. She walks by a line of homeless people waiting to eat at a soup kitchen. Someone touches her on the arm and Molly, frightened, turns to see who it is.

The old woman says, "Remember me, Child? I'm Glad, and you tripped over my foot. Isn't your name Polly?"

"Molly, and I was just coming to check on you, Glad!" she replies.

"Well, my foot is just fine, Honey. Are you hungry? You can be my lunch guest here at Hunger's Kitchen."

Molly pauses, and Glad continues, "It's free, of course, but it's pretty good food. I'd really appreciate your company." With this, Molly relents and gets in line. Molly believes it's time she starts making some friends, and Glad seems special.

The line is moving slowly, and they make polite conversation, touching on subjects such as the weather, and air quality. Finally, they get inside the building to the food table, and it does look good. They both get baked chicken, mashed potatoes, salad, a piece of apple pie, and milk to drink. The dining room is getting crowded and Glad doesn't walk very fast, but they find a couple of seats across from each other. Glad bows her head for a brief time and then begins to eat. Molly doesn't know what to do, so she waits to start eating when Glad starts. She feels this is the respectful thing to do. They both comment on how tasty the food is.

"Where are you from, Molly?" Glad asks.

"Not too far from here, Glad, but I don't have any family except a brother named Jason, and I can't find him," Molly responds. Glad inquires as to why her brother is lost, and Molly, reluctantly, tells her the story and assures Glad that she never stops looking for him. They take a break between lunch and dessert, and Glad asks about Molly's work and college. Molly relates how she recently got the triple whammy--lost her job, left her boyfriend, and became instantly homeless. However, she also tells Glad how lucky she was to get into a shelter that same evening. Molly's pleased that it's so easy to talk with Glad, and is horribly curious about how a sweet person like her could end up on the streets. There's a pause in the conversation, and Molly jumps right in.

"Glad, how is it that a lovely woman like you ends up on the streets homeless?"

Glad looks down for a few seconds to collect her thoughts, looks up at Molly and replies, "Child, I'm more disenfranchised than homeless. It's a long story that I'll go into someday, but for now I'm getting tired and need to go check on my old friend, Axel."

Molly drops her napkin on the floor and bends down to pick it up. She notices that Glad's ankles are mildly swollen, but she doesn't feel comfortable asking about this yet. She stands up, extends her hand to Glad and says, "Come on, Glad. I'll walk you home." Glad wraps a piece of chicken in a napkin for Axel and puts it in her pocket, Molly helps her up, and they leave.

They have about three blocks to walk, but Glad is very slow. She stops a couple of times--once to greet an old man named Ernie, and another time to greet a middle-aged woman named Shelly.

Molly finally asks, "How long have you been homeless, Glad?"

"Eight long years."

"Here in Brooklyn?--I don't know how you survive the winters. It makes me shiver just to think about it," Molly says.

"It's very hard, Honey, but somehow Axel and I pull through. If I'm lucky, I can move my box next to a heat vent by one of these buildings. On really cold days, I go to the library," Glad responds.

"I see, Glad. The public library is heated and has rest-rooms," Molly says, and then continues. "I never thought I'd find myself in this situation, and I'm really struggling with the stigma attached to being homeless."

Glad responds, "Everyday, you hold your head up with dignity and, if necessary, you advise people that's how you want to be treated. Just about everyone is down on their luck at times."

Molly starts to develop feelings of admiration and respect for Glad, and wonders if this is what having a grandmother feels like. Her family was very fragmented, so she never knew her grandparents very well. Her grandmother was distant, even though Molly lived with her for almost two years.

The two women walk the last block in silence as they survey all the poverty, sorrow, and hopelessness around them. It's easy to see why some of these poor souls are victimized.

They reach Glad's home, where Axel sits, waiting. Glad gives him the piece of chicken, and he tears into it wholeheartedly.

She then touches Molly's arm and says, "I know it's tough at first, Molly, but there are opportunities each day to find inner strength and resolve. Look for the opportunities, and don't give up."

"Oh, Glad," Molly laments, "I just feel so vulnerable--I can't relax or enjoy hardly anything."

"Your body has protective mechanisms, Child--don't ignore your gut feelings; listen to them," Glad advises. "You seem to have good instincts, Molly. Set your mind to surviving twenty-four hours at a time. It helps to break things down into manageable pieces."

"That puts things into perspective, Glad. Thanks for the sound advice," Molly says, suddenly feeling better.

Glad looks tired and needs to get off her feet. Molly needs to go hit the books. She checks her phone and it's after 2:00 p.m., so she can study at the shelter—in accordance with the ground rules. Molly reflects on the afternoon and thinks Glad is so spunky and cute, she'd like to call her *Mrs. T.* For Molly, it's a term of endearment.

Molly asks, "Glad, would you mind horribly if I call you *Mrs. T*? It seems spunky--like your personality." Glad considers this for a few seconds and then agrees. Molly wants to hug her, but thinks it might be a little premature. She vows that for the rest of the semester, she'll have lunch with Mrs. T at least every Wednesday, and will check on her as much as she can.

Before Molly leaves, Mrs. T says, "There's one more thing, Molly."

"What, Mrs. T?" she inquires.

"I've enjoyed my time with you so much, would you mind if I give you a hug?" Mrs. T asks.

Molly says, "Not at all, and thank you for the wonderful company and lunch." As they share a gentle hug, neither of them realizes that this is the beginning of a warm, caring relationship.

6

THE PROMOTION

Lucy catches Molly as she's finishing breakfast and asks, "Molly, would you keep an eye on things while I run to the pharmacy to pick up a prescription? I shouldn't be gone more than 15 minutes."

"Sure, Lucy," Molly says as Lucy's on her way out the door.

Lucy pops her head back in and says, "Oh, would you please check on Jackie? She didn't eat breakfast."

"I'll go right now," Molly replies, and heads down the hall.

Molly helps Lucy as much as she can and feels good that Lucy trusts her. Confidentiality is paramount to Molly, too. Also, she might be able to turn these extra duties into a management internship for school. Who knows? She's keeping a journal, in case she decides to discuss it with Lucy. When Molly walks into the sleeping room, she notices that Jackie's back in bed. Calling her name, she approaches Jackie's cot and hears her moan deeply.

"Jackie, are you OK?" Molly asks. She kneels next to the cot to face Jackie, who is wet with perspiration and has a grimace on her face.

"I think I'm in early labor," Jackie volunteers, "and my back hurts so bad."

Molly inquires, "Do you have any pain in your gut?"

"Yes, I have cramping and the bed feels wet."

Alarmed, Molly asks if she can check her, and Jackie agrees. Molly helps Jackie roll from her side onto her back and pulls the covers down so she can see between Jackie's legs--being careful to respect her privacy. There's fluid leaking from Jackie's vagina and some blood-tinged mucous on the sheet. Jackie moans when she starts cramping again.

"How often are you having cramps?" Molly asks.

Jackie looks at the clock on the wall and replies, "About every 10 minutes."

Molly pulls her cell phone out of her pocket and tells Jackie that she's dialing 911. When the dispatcher answers, Molly tells her what's going on and the dispatcher requests that a paramedic unit be sent. In the interim, Molly tries to comfort Jackie while gathering up all of Jackie's belongings. If Jackie has the baby, she won't be coming back to Alma de Lucy. Molly writes her cell phone number on a piece of paper and puts it in Jackie's pocket.

"Here's my phone number. If you have your little baby, please call and let me know so I can tell everyone."

"OK, Molly," Jackie answers, "and thank you so much for helping me."

"I'm happy to help," Molly says, and touches Jackie's hand.

They hear sirens close by and Molly says, "I'll go see if that's the paramedics." She motions for another guest to go over and watch Jackie.

Lucy arrives just as the paramedics are loading Jackie into the ambulance. She asks Molly if Jackie went into labor.

"I'm not a nurse," Molly responds, "but I believe so. I checked Jackie and dialed 911 right away. Jackie has back pain, abdominal cramping, and fluid leaking from her vagina. She's four weeks early, and I felt the doctors should check her."

"You did the right thing," Lucy says, as she and Molly walk into the shelter.

Molly grabs her things for school--she'll have to hurry to be there on time. On her way, she prays that Jackie will be OK. She'll have to see Mrs. T after class, and if her studies permit, maybe she can have lunch with her. She can't wait to tell Mrs. T about her exciting morning. Molly and Mrs. T have become very close--she's the grandmother Molly never had, and Molly's very protective of her. It doesn't matter that Mrs. T is white and Molly's half black--the thought never entered her mind.

A couple of times on weekends, Molly borrowed the shelter wheelchair and took Mrs. T to free street fares. She got Mrs. T a cherry snow cone and stopped at a public restroom on the way back to Mrs. T's house. Mrs. T has a birthday coming up soon, and Molly thinks about what she can do to make it special. She'll have to go shopping at the thrift store. Considering that she doesn't have a job, Molly wonders how she got so busy.

After Molly's finance class, she's really in a crunch--the professor assigned a short paper discussing functional vs. dysfunctional components of budget principles for discussion next week. Molly has a B average in this class, so she needs to do well. Unfortunately, she'll have to write this over the weekend. She heads for the library to search for references. Then she'll stop by to see Mrs. T.

In the library, Molly boots up her laptop to access her e-mail--*no time for social media today*, she thinks. Molly and Don are carrying on an e-mail correspondence, but haven't seen each other for almost a week. She recently told him that she can only handle friendship at this time, and he's giving her a lot of latitude, but she wonders how long that will last.

Molly would love to tell Don the truth about her situation but is torn by ambivalence. She's determined that she likes him and wonders why she has mixed emotions. But her life is on *overwhelm* right now, and she's afraid to add emotional involvement to the equation--look what happened with Jackson. Molly's e-mail signals that she has a new message, and it's from Don. *Wow, he's thinking about me at the same time I'm thinking about him*, Molly muses. Don wants to know when she can stop by the shop so he and Jasper can see her. Molly responds that she'll stop by for a short visit at the end of the day. She hesitates before she writes, "I'll be glad to see you guys, too!" Then she begins a search for references for her paper. She won't have much time to visit with Mrs. T today, either.

When Molly leaves the library, she goes directly to Mrs. T's house and finds her sitting in a rickety lawn chair with Axel at her feet. Her ankles are still puffy, and she doesn't look as well as she did yesterday.

"I'm going to have to find you a footstool to put your feet up on," Molly says as she hugs her.

She sits down on the pavement, puts her carry-on in front of Mrs. T, and says "Here, use this for now." Axel rubs against Molly's leg, and she pets him. Molly advises Mrs. T that she doesn't have much time because she promised to go see Don and Jasper before she goes to the shelter to study. Mrs. T and Don know about each other, but haven't met yet. However, her intuition is right on target believing that Molly is sweet on Don--Molly just needs to figure it out herself.

She looks at Molly and says, "Well, I sure hope that man makes an honest woman out of you someday soon. You're sweet on him, Child, and you need to stop stringing him along."

Molly isn't shocked by this message--that's one thing she loves about Mrs. T; she's blatantly honest. She shows Mrs. T how adept she is at changing the subject when she tells her all about the exciting morning at the shelter. Then she has to leave for a short visit with the guys at the coffee house. Molly wonders what kind of dreamy concoction Don will make for her this time. Her thoughts drift back to Mrs. T. Molly feels uneasy about her condition and realizes she will have to get her some medical attention soon.

As Molly approaches the coffee shop, Jasper starts jumping and barking--he recognizes her footsteps now. She pets him as soon as she enters and pulls a biscuit from her bag. She found a box of stale biscuits at the discount store, but Jasper doesn't mind that they're stale--he loves treats from Molly. Don is delighted, greets Molly with a formal hug, and hands her a cappuccino. They sit down to chat and Molly updates him on Mrs. T and her new school assignment.

Don advises Molly that he's been invited to a business management internship for two weeks at the University of

New Hampshire, but he isn't sure he can get full coverage at the shop.

"Wow, Don, that sounds like a super opportunity," Molly acknowledges, "but what about Jasper?"

"If I'm unable to take Jasper, I assure you he'll have a good sitter at home," Don replies.

Molly's not sure how she feels about him leaving for two weeks and she wonders who this *good sitter* is. After about 45 minutes, Molly reluctantly tells Don that she has to go study. She gets her bag, says goodbye, and as she's going out the door yells, "I'll e-mail you."

Don stands in the doorway and sighs--he so wants to kiss her.

When Molly gets to the shelter, she immediately finds Lucy and asks, "Lucy, have we heard anything from Jackie yet?"

"No, there's been no word," Lucy pauses. "Molly, if you have a few minutes, I'd like to talk with you after supper."

Molly agrees, "Sure, Lucy, no problem." She goes to the sleeping room to stash her things, wondering what's up. Hopefully, Lucy isn't going to remind her that her 30 days expire next week.

Lucy returns to the kitchen to work on supper. She's looking forward to her discussion with Molly later. Molly has become almost indispensable to Lucy and has made her life so much easier. Molly does extra chores, runs errands on her way to and from school, talks with and counsels other guests when they're depressed or distraught, and respects confidentiality. A couple of the more withdrawn women have even spoken with Molly. Lucy feels it was fate that brought Molly to them--she has great people skills and, above all, she has compassion. For these reasons, Lucy plans to offer Molly full-time status at the end of her 30 days and hopes she'll stay on at Alma de Lucy.

After supper, when things are put away and the helpers are doing the dishes, Lucy finds Molly studying in the sleeping room.

"May I sit on the foot of your bed, Molly?" Lucy asks.

"Sure." Molly gestures with her hand toward the foot of the bed.

Lucy begins with, "Molly, I don't know how to thank you for all of your assistance." She reviews with Molly all that she does to help and how her presence positively impacts the shelter, and especially the guests.

"Thanks, Lucy, but you've really got your hands full, and I enjoy helping."

Lucy continues, "Molly, things run better when you're here, and I want you to stay on at Alma de Lucy, full-time."

Molly perks up. "What do you mean, Lucy?"

"I want you to be my assistant manager and stay here. Of course, your salary will be room and board. What do you think, Molly?"

Molly squeals with delight. "This is great--I really enjoy being here and helping. You've just solved a huge problem for me, as I haven't been able to find work."

"I take it you're saying yes?" Lucy inquires with a grin.

"Yes, most definitely yes," Molly says. "Thank you for the opportunity, Lucy."

Lucy stands up, "We'll work out the details tomorrow, and I'll make the announcement at dinner. I just wish I knew where you get all of your energy, Molly. You're amazing!"

Molly shakes her hand and smiles. As Lucy starts to leave the room, her cell phone rings. She stops to talk, grins when she hangs up, and motions to Molly to follow her to the living room. All of the guests are watching TV, playing cards, and talking.

Lucy walks to the front of the room and says, "Ladies, I have an announcement. It's a boy--Levi Andrew Barnes!" Everyone cheers.

7

ALLI IN THE ALLEY

Molly is more relaxed since she was given full-time status at Alma de Lucy. Plus, she was finally granted unemployment benefits by the state, so she isn't so edgy. Continuing to look for a job, she follows up with many places a second time, but it's so hard on her school schedule. Today she doesn't have class until 1:00 p.m., so she's on her way to the thrift store to look for a birthday gift for Mrs. T--without a clue as to what to buy. When she gets to the store, she starts to cruise the aisles in search of a special gift. Molly feels strongly that it needs to be something classy, because Mrs. T is so dignified. Sifting through a box of costume jewelry, she finds a pair of designer earrings that are silver-toned squares with a lion logo. She holds them up and thinks, "This is it--she adores cats! I can polish these earrings right up." She purchases the earrings for $2.00, puts them in her backpack, and takes off to see Mrs. T.

When Molly arrives at Mrs. T's abode, she finds her resting in her box. Molly helps Mrs. T up and notices that she's slightly short of breath and that her ankles are moderately swollen. The two ladies hug and Molly says, "You seem to be a little short of breath, Mrs. T. How do you feel?"

"I just feel tired, Child--I don't have any energy,"

Molly tells Mrs. T that she's going to see if she can borrow a wheelchair from someone and take her to the free clinic.

"You need medication, Mrs. T." Molly leaves to look for a chair. In about 10 minutes she comes back with a wheelchair she borrowed from a Mr. Reed, near the end of the block. There's a bungee cord on the chair and Molly is able to affix her bag--she can't leave it or she might not see it again. She helps Mrs. T into the chair, and away they go.

At the City Clinic, Molly helps Mrs. T fill out some paperwork. It's a good thing Mrs. T has a chair--there isn't a vacant seat anywhere. Mrs. T dozes off and on during the 45-minute wait before a nurse comes to the door and calls her name. Molly pushes the chair into the nurses' area where Mrs. T is weighed and has her blood pressure, pulse and temperature checked. After reviewing Mrs. T's medical history form, the nurse puts Molly and Mrs. T in an exam room. A few minutes later a young Dr. Rollin Clark comes in to examine Mrs. T. He seems quite thorough and treats her with respect. Dr. Clark explains to Mrs. T that her heart isn't working efficiently as a pump because it's wearing out, and he's going to put her on a little digitalis to strengthen it. He knows he can't prescribe water pills to an elderly woman living on the street--she'd never make it to a bathroom in time. So Dr. Clark advises her not to salt her food, orders a chest X-ray, an EKG, and some blood work, and says he wants to see her again in two weeks. Molly takes Mrs. T to complete all of the tests and picks up the prescription at the clinic pharmacy. As she's wheeling her out of the clinic, Mrs. T casually remarks, "I'm going to put salt on my eggs--I don't like eggs without salt." Molly smiles and pats her on the shoulder.

Class is over and Molly heads for the library. She wants to research digitalis so she can help Mrs. T. Molly learns a lot--digitalis is derived from a plant called foxglove, and it's poisonous. *Yipes!* Molly thinks, and then notes that the patient's pulse needs to be checked daily and should be 60 beats or more per minute. She thinks Mrs. T can remember to take her pill, but Molly will have to check her pulse. *There's so much to consider when there are health issues*, Molly muses. She so wishes Mrs. T could move into the shelter, but Lucy might not take Axel--and what would happen at the end of 30 days?

With a lot on her mind, Molly winds up her research and leaves the campus. She stops by to briefly check on Mrs. T and informs her that she shouldn't take her digitalis until Molly gets there to check her pulse every morning. Mrs. T says she understands and tells Molly she's going to take a nap--this day has just done her in. Molly hugs her and takes off for the shelter to study. It's time she wrote the budget discussion for her finance class next week.

Transit time is daily Review and Resolution time for Molly-- her *R & R*. Today she's grateful that Lucy gave her a key to the shelter so she can now move around *carte blanche*. With Molly's ever-changing schedule, it helps immensely, and she feels blessed in the way things are working out. Also, she's met some incredible, kind, considerate, selfless people she never would have met if she wasn't homeless. Lucy is an icon, she adores Mrs. T, Rudy is her sage, and Don-- what about Don? She can't deny that warm feeling she gets when she thinks about him, talks with him, or sees him. "OK, I'll admit I have a crush on Don," she says aloud, and then smiles. Molly really likes him and they have a lot in common, but she's not ready to spill her guts to him about her situation. She's friendly, but remains reserved while she's searching her soul for answers.

Molly's route between school and the shelter is working well--there are no adverse events to report. Near the shelter, though, she walks by an alley where she hears what sounds like a moan. Two feet are sticking out from behind a dumpster, and Molly goes to investigate. A woman is lying beside the dumpster with dirty clothes, matted hair, and blood on the side of her face--she probably cut her face when she fell or was thrown there and possibly left to die. The woman continues to moan, is sweating profusely, has a runny nose and is holding her gut. Molly can see her chest rise and fall when she breathes and stoops down to look at her wounded face. She tilts the woman's face upward and gasps--its Alli, Rudy's sister. Molly swings into rescue mode, takes out her phone to call Lucy, and asks for permission to bring the woman to the shelter.

Lucy responds, "Oh, Molly, you know we're full, and having someone here who's detoxing is so disruptive."

"But haven't at least a third of your guests been through this? It may be a great environment for Alli."

"Alli? Alli who?" Lucy asks.

"Allison Lee--Rudy's sister. She's conscious but confused, and has a cut on the side of her face."

"OK, this one's for Rudy," Lucy responds. "Will you be able to get her here?"

"I'll try. I'll call you back if I have a difficult time," Molly says and hangs up. She has a hard time getting Alli out from beside the dumpster, but Alli is able to stand--she's wobbly, but she can stand. "This is going to be slow going," Molly mutters under her breath, as she puts Alli's arm on her shoulder and slips an arm around Alli's waist. Then she thinks, *whatever Rudy did for Lucy must be something really big.*

It takes over half an hour to walk the two blocks to the shelter, with a *passenger* hanging on, and two bags. Molly is so relieved when she reaches Alma de Lucy that she calls for help at the front door, and a couple of guests run out to assist.

"Please give her some first aid for her face right away," Molly urges. "I'll fix her a pallet on the floor, but then I need to talk with Lucy." Molly gets a blanket and small pillow, pulls the carpet tiles out from under her cot, and creates a pallet in her old corner.

Lucy is in the kitchen finishing some prep work for dinner when Molly finds her. They grab some coffee and go into the dining room for a break. Molly tells Lucy how she met Alli and how close Alli and Rudy are. She volunteers to assist Alli with the intake paperwork the next day. Then Molly tells Lucy about the rest of her unbelievable day--it's amazing she can squeeze school in. Since Molly became Lucy's assistant, their relationship has become more personal and close--almost like sisters--and they work well together as a team.

Alli is moving into the late stages of withdrawal and starts to vomit and have diarrhea. It's apparent she OD'd on smack. Molly gets up and assists Alli for about four hours during the night. She finally becomes so exhausted she doesn't hear Alli any longer, so a couple of guests get up to help. It's like angels fluttering around Alli to set things right. Molly sleeps deeply for three hours before she has to get up. Alli is finally sleeping peacefully in the corner, looking pale and fragile. Lucy has promised to watch Alli while Molly tends to Mrs. T and goes to school.

Molly eats a little breakfast, cleans up, and leaves early. She's not a bundle of energy today, that's for sure, but she is resolved, and she'll make it. Tomorrow is Mrs. T's 78th birthday and Molly needs to make a card tonight and find two cupcakes in the morning. Mrs. T is sitting in her lawn chair with Axel on her lap and smiles when Molly arrives. She looks a little better today, and she's less short of breath. Molly checks her pulse and it's 70, so Mrs. T can take her digitalis. Molly then tells Mrs. T about Alli and that she'll have to cut their visits short for a couple of days so she can help Alli.

"Don't worry, though, Mrs. T," Molly says. "Tomorrow looks very good for being a special day."

"Oh, Child, don't go to any trouble tomorrow--you're so busy," Mrs. T replies.

"We'll see about that tomorrow," Molly says as she gives Mrs. T a goodbye hug and kiss.

"I've got to scoot to school," she says, and takes off.

As soon as class is over, Molly decides to call Rudy and tell him what has happened to Alli. He answers his phone and greets her with, "Hi, Miss Molly."

"Rudy, I'm glad I caught you. There's something very important that I need to tell you about." Molly tells him about the events of yesterday and how Alli is doing.

"I tried to call her this morning and was worried when she didn't answer," Rudy says.

Molly replies, "Now that you mention it, Alli didn't have a cell phone on her when she came to the shelter--it may be lost. On my way home today, I'll go back to the alley where I found her and see if I can locate it."

Rudy thanks Molly, and inquires further, "What's going to happen to Alli? Can she stay at the shelter?"

Molly advises Rudy that Lucy said Alli can stay at the shelter for the standard 30 days. Also, Molly's going to work with Alli and try to ensure that she makes all of her meetings.

"This environment may be good for Alli--some of the guests at Alma de Lucy have walked in Alli's shoes and can be supportive and helpful," Molly tells Rudy. "It may be the best thing for her, Rudy. Have faith."

"My faith has been worn a little thin, Molly, but I admire your optimism."

"Well, you don't seem ready to abandon her, Rudy," Molly replies.

"Oh God, no," Rudy blurts out. "I'll never give up hope. When may I see Alli?"

Molly explains that she's going back to the shelter to help Alli with the intake paperwork. She'll advise Alli that she called him and let Alli decide when she's ready to see Rudy. Alli has got to get herself together and develop some resolve.

Molly tells Rudy, "It will be good for her to be in charge of that decision--hopefully she won't feel as much shame when she faces you, Rudy."

"I understand, Molly, and my faith is in you," Rudy says, "but will you call me every day and tell me how she's doing?"

"Sure, Rudy, and I'll tell you about her progress. I know you're a great source of moral support and love for Alli. For now, let's be patient!" Molly counsels. Rudy feels more hopeful, says goodbye to Molly, and thanks God for his wonderful new friend.

8

LIFE IS A GIFT

Molly's *R & R* time has pretty much come to an end for this trip back to the shelter. She's standing at the entrance of the alley where she found Alli yesterday. It appears to be vacant, so she goes down to the dumpster to search for Alli's phone. She picks up a stick so she can sift through the trash if she needs to, but when she kneels down by the corner of the dumpster, she hears a faint beep. She looks under the dumpster and sees a green light flashing. *Hopefully, it's only Rudy's voicemail and not a dealer,* Molly thinks as she reaches under the dumpster to retrieve it.

When Molly gets to the shelter, she finds Alli in the dining room having tea and toast. She's all disheveled, pale, and so shaky she has difficulty getting the teacup back on the saucer. "Hi, Alli! It's good to see you up and moving. How are you feeling?" Molly inquires.

"Oh, embarrassed, ashamed, disgusted, and I can't remember a thing," Alli replies. She looks up at Molly and a light goes off. "Hey, you're Rudy's friend--Polly?"

"I'm Molly," she responds, "and I live here, too. Have you met Lucy Mercado?"

"Yes, she seems like a nice lady. Lucy said that you'll be helping me with some paperwork. I'd like to stay here, Molly, and I understand it's only for 30 days."

"I'll get the paperwork and help you. Alli, I'm the one who found you in the alley and brought you here. You really scared us, but we stayed with you all night," Molly says as she gets the paperwork out of a bin on the wall and sits back down.

"Thank you, Molly; I'm so depressed," Alli says and begins to cry.

"Those are tears of remorse, Alli," Molly replies with compassion. "Many women here have cried them and have been where you are today." Alli doesn't make eye contact, but Molly can tell that she's listening.

Molly continues, "If you want to get clean, healthy, and enjoy life again, landing here is a great opportunity. You'll need to make all of your meetings, but we'll help you."

"Thank you, Molly," Alli says as she extends a shaky hand. Molly takes it, and shakes it warmly.

Molly advises Alli, "By the way, I did call Rudy this morning and let him know what has happened to you. He's grateful you're here and wants you to call him when you're ready for a visit. If you don't mind, I'll keep him posted on your progress. He is very concerned."

"That sounds like a good plan, Molly. Thanks!" Alli says.

Molly walks Alli through the intake paperwork, and because Alli's so shaky, Molly fills in the blanks for her and has Alli sign at the bottom. She and Alli review the rules, and Molly gives her the old, *sorry you have to sleep on the floor,* speech. Alli is guarded, but likes Molly and believes she's genuinely concerned. With Rudy as a common thread, Alli feels more relaxed with Molly and decides to confide in her.

Alli has an eight year-old son named Seth. She wasn't able to provide for him a couple of years ago after his father took off. CPS took Seth away from her and placed him in a foster home.

"They took the love of my life--my freckle-faced, soccer-crazed son," Alli relates. She's exhausted trying to battle the system, and feels she can't do anything right. It breaks her heart that she's not allowed to see Seth; she became very depressed and turned to drugs as an escape.

"I know it's wrong, but I'm hooked and have been unable to stop using," Alli laments.

Molly looks at Alli and says, "You're clean today, and it's up to you to decide to be clean tomorrow, and the next day, and the next. It's your choice, Alli."

"I need strength, Molly."

"And where are you going to find that strength, Alli? It looks to me like your reserves are depleted. Maybe that's a good place to start--building up your inner reserves," Molly suggests.

Alli replies, "I don't know where to start."

"Well, I'm not a substance abuse counselor, Alli--I'm pretty much shooting from the hip," Molly continues. "But it seems that a good place for you to start would be here at Alma de Lucy. Perhaps being here is a gift you've been given--we'll all help you, Alli, but you've got to do the work, and it will be very hard."

"I'll get back into my recovery group tomorrow," Alli responds.

"That will be a good start, Alli, and Lucy may have some bus vouchers," Molly advises. "Ask around, maybe someone here would like to go with you. What are you going to do today?"

Alli responds, "I'm going to get cleaned up and begin to make a list of what I have to be grateful for."

"That sounds like a small journey on the road back to Seth," Molly approves, "and a great way to start building reserves. If you're going to challenge CPS, you'll need lots of reserves."

"Thanks again, Molly. Your advice is very sound and encouraging," Alli says with a slight smile.

"With your permission, I'll hang onto your cell phone for now. You may consider changing your number. Also, Rudy said he left you a message yesterday morning," Molly says.

Alli reflects, "I'm grateful that I have such a loving brother. You may hang onto my phone, Molly."

"OK, it sounds like a plan. Now, if you'll excuse me, I've got a dear friend with a birthday today and I've got to go buy some cupcakes for a celebration," Molly says as she leaves.

"Good luck, Molly," Alli says.

Molly looks back and smiles.

Then, as Molly runs out the door: "Holy shish kabob," Molly yells. "Mrs. T is 78 years old today!"

Lucy gave Molly a candle. She wrapped the earrings in the newspaper comics because they're so colorful, and then tied her gift with a piece of string. On the way to see Mrs. T, Molly finds a bakery and buys two day-old cupcakes for fifty cents--what luck!

When Molly arrives at Mrs. T's house, she's up in her chair with her hair all combed and Axel on her lap.

"First things first," Molly says as she kisses Mrs. T and puts her fingers on her wrist to check her pulse. After Mrs. T swallows her digitalis pill, Molly breaks out in the Happy Birthday song and dances around Mrs. T's chair. Axel looks at her like he suspects she's finally lost it. Then Molly sits down on the sidewalk, gets into her backpack for the homemade card and the gift. Molly had drawn colorful butterflies on the card and written "Happy Birthday to a great lady." Inside the card she wrote a little poem:

In my heart, you're a star,
and the Grandmother I never knew.

Life is a journey that will take us far,
simply because I Love You.

Happy Birthday, Mrs. T!
Love, Molly

Mrs. T is quiet for a minute and then says, "That's a very special message, Molly. I'd be proud to have you as a grand-daughter." Molly gets up and hugs Mrs. T, thanks her, and then gives her the little gift.

"Oh, Child, what have you done?" Mrs. T exclaims.

"Open it, open it," Molly says. Mrs. T opens the package to find the pair of lion-faced earrings.

"These are beautiful, Molly. I've always preferred silver to gold. Here, help me put them on." Molly puts them on her and shows her a mirror. Mrs. T is beaming.

"They look so sophisticated, and Axel likes them, too. Thank you, Honey."

Then Molly produces the cupcakes from a bag and puts a candle on Mrs. T's cupcake. However, they don't have a match to light it, so they just eat the cupcakes.

Mrs. T asks, "How is it that you chose butterflies for the front of my card?"

"I love butterflies myself--they're so colorful and care-free, and they create a feeling of joy," Molly replies.

Mrs. T relates a story to Molly about her eighth birthday. Her mother could draw and paint wonderful pictures, and for some reason she made a special cake for Mrs. T's eighth birthday and painted beautiful butterflies all over the top.

"It was magical," Mrs. T said with a nostalgic look in her eyes. "I didn't want my mother to cut it, but we did, of course--when the yearning for that chocolate became too much to bear. But I'll never forget that beautiful cake."

"What a wonderful story, Mrs. T. Thanks for sharing it with me," Molly says. She feels very privileged since it's the first time Mrs. T has told her something personal. Mrs. T displays a big smile, but can't stop yawning.

"Well, the birthday girl looks tired," Molly says. "I'll let you have a nice nap while I go study. I'm so far behind in my studies--with everything that's been going on at the shelter. Do you mind, Mrs. T?"

"Oh, no, Child, your studies are very important," Mrs. T responds. Once again, she thanks Molly for everything. "I'll never forget this day, Molly. You're a special girl, and you're going to go places--I just know it," Mrs. T says.

"Thanks for the kind words. I'll see you in the morning, Mrs. T, and Happy Birthday again," Molly says as she hugs and kisses Mrs. T goodbye.

Molly's in her *R & R* mode when she walks to the shelter. She feels a dichotomy between the strength she exhibits when she helps people versus the strength she really feels she has. *Maybe I need to check my reserves*, she thinks. She hasn't seen or heard from Don in a couple of days, and suddenly she can't get him off her mind. He always seems to have the proper perspective about things. Molly's life is filled with so much tension, she thinks it would feel like a vacation to sit down and visit with Don. *My studies will just have to wait*, Molly thinks as she takes out her phone and gives him a call.

"Been too long," he answers.

"I thought that was Bean Too Long," Molly replies.

"Not in your case, it's *been* too long," he responds.

Molly chuckles. "If you don't have a class tonight, are you up for a spontaneous visit?"

"Jasper and I are in luck then, because I don't have school. We would welcome a visit," Don responds.

Molly changes her course and realizes she's wearing a warm smile on her face. She's looking forward to seeing Don and Jasper, and is hoping for a much-needed hug from Don.

For his part, Don knows his feelings for Molly are strong, but he has decided to let her come to him. He hopes it's working, because she's making him crazy! He starts to make two white chocolate lattes.

When Molly arrives at the coffee shop, Jasper is by the door. "How cute you are," Molly says as she hands him a biscuit and bends down to pet him.

"Boy, he's the lucky guy," Don says as he puts the lattes on a table. "I'm jealous!"

"Sorry, but how can I ignore all of his enthusiasm?" Molly says. She approaches Don and gives him a hug that's a little more casual and warm than past hugs.

Don grins and motions for Molly to sit down. She tastes her latte and says, "Ummm, maestro. Thanks!"

"At your service!" he replies, with a slight bow. "So tell me how you're doing and what's going on." Molly describes her last two days, starting with Mrs. T's health challenges and her birthday celebration--including the personal story about the cake Mrs. T's mom made her for her eighth birthday.

These aren't exactly hot conversational topics, but Don's a good listener and Molly appreciates his attentive listening style. Sometimes he reflects Molly's thoughts back to her and she becomes more introspective. Molly likes that--it broadens her perspective at times. Then she inquires about Don's potential internship at the University of New Hampshire.

"Well, I decided against it because I heard about another internship that's local, and probably more applicable to what I need," Don relates.

"How is it more applicable? What kind of internship are you interested in?" Molly realizes how little she knows about Don's program.

"For starters--other than the convenience of the program being local--I'm interested in business development, marketing and branding. The local internship concentrates on these areas, plus I'll get course credit," Don says.

Molly comments, "Course credit is a huge benefit."

"But here's the kicker," Don continues. "Once a week, there's a business roundtable with local speakers. Who wouldn't want an opportunity to meet and network with successful businesspeople from the community? I could make some valuable contacts for the future."

"What a great opportunity. Good luck, Don." She feels happy for him and thinks, *He's so passionate about everything he does.*

"Oh, I got my application in right away. I'll let you know when I hear something," Don responds. "Now, what else is going on with you?"

Molly finally feels comfortable enough to tell him about her ordeal with Alli.

Don's amazed and inquires, "What did you do? Was she dying?"

"No, she was conscious and moaning--her respirations were fairly normal. So, with some difficulty, I managed to get her to a local shelter for women," Molly says.

"Do you know how she's doing?" Don asks. He keeps his eyes on Molly as she speaks.

Molly replies, "I checked on her today and she was up--trying to get some nourishment. She looked a mess and was very shaky, but she made it." Molly then adds, "I spoke with her and agreed to notify her brother about her condition and where she's staying, which I did."

"Wow, Molly, you may have saved her life," Don says.

"Well, I certainly hope she can use this event to get her life in order," Molly responds, as she looks at the clock. "We've been talking for over an hour and I have a finance paper to finish," she announces. "I'd better get going."

"Darn," Don says, "I never lack for interesting conversation around here, but yours is the best."

Molly grins and replies, "Keep going--I love flattery."

"How much?" Don asks with a sly smile. "Enough to go to the park with Jasper and me on Sunday for a picnic?"

This catches Molly off guard. "I don't know. I have to go to the library to finish my paper. Can you pick me up there?"

At least she isn't declining, Don thinks. He still knows nothing about where she lives and whether she lives with someone. He decides to be patient a little longer, and says, "Why don't we shoot for around 1:00 p.m.? You can call me fifteen minutes before you can be out by the curb in front of the library."

"It's a date," Molly says as she gives him a goodbye hug and takes off. "See you Sunday!"

It's about time, Don thinks, with excitement welling up in his chest. He looks at Jasper and says, "I think I'm getting somewhere with the beautiful wench, Master Jasper." Jasper gives him the perfunctory yelp. "Come on, let's plan a special picnic. If life is a *gift,* I'm loving the *present,*" Don says with a smile.

9

THE 'REAL' DONALD

What does *Dr. Clark mean by* "fairly stable?" Molly wonders as she looks in the sleeping room mirror to put on her blush. She took Mrs. T to the clinic for her follow-up visit, and after his examination, that's what Dr. Clark said. It must be shades of gray between stable and unstable. She'll have to keep a close eye on Mrs. T, as she feels tired most of the time. Their special trips to free events are starting to dwindle. Molly applies lip gloss and takes one last look at her hair, just as Alli enters the room.

"Oh, there you are Molly. Have you got a couple of minutes?"

"Sure, Alli! What's up?" Molly responds.

Alli offers her a smile. "Well, I have some good news for a change. First, I've signed up to volunteer at St. Anthony's Food Bank two days a week."

"That's great news, Alli. I hear they're a good group to work with."

Alli continues, "Also, I thought you'd like to know that I'm going to see Rudy this afternoon. I finally feel ready to face him, and I believe it's time I apologize for all the heartache I've caused him."

Molly gives Alli a hug and says, "This is wonderful, Alli, and I'm so glad you're taking positive action. That must take a lot of courage."

"It's downright scary, but I'm taking baby steps. You're right; landing here at Alma de Lucy is a great opportunity for me. I don't know how I'll ever repay everyone," Alli responds.

Molly replies, "Just get healthy and fit. That would be reward enough."

"Thanks, Molly. I can't wait to tell Rudy. I'll let you know how it goes," Alli says as she heads for the door.

"*Wow, that girl's a real whirlwind without drugs,*" Molly says to herself as she picks up her backpack to go to the library. Lucy lets her put her rolling bag in a locked closet when she needs to, such as today. That would be way too much baggage for a picnic. One last look at her appearance in the mirror, and Molly, too, is out the door. She knows she looks pretty; she even ironed her blouse for the occasion. So why is she so nervous about a date with Don? *I'm not even going there,* Molly thinks. She needs to go see Mrs. T first and check her pulse, and then go to the library. Molly does notice that it's a beautiful day with sunny skies, moderate weather, and a mild breeze. *What a great day for a picnic!* she thinks, and smiles.

❧

Mrs. T is in her chair dozing and Axel is curled up in the box when Molly arrives. Molly checks her pulse, and Mrs. T wakes up. "How are you feeling today, Mrs. T?" Molly asks with a hug.

"Oh, Child, I think I'm outliving my warranty," Mrs. T responds.

"Let me see that warranty!" Molly teases.

Mrs. T looks up and asks, "Do I have to take this medicine, Molly? It makes me feel so tired."

"That's a good question for Dr. Clark. I'll stop by the clinic this week and ask," Molly replies, as she hands Mrs. T some water to take her pill.

Mrs. T looks Molly over and remarks, "My, you look extra pretty today, Child. It's a beautiful day for a picnic, too."

"I'm nervous, but I'm looking forward to it," Molly says.

"Just be your lovely self, Molly, and have a wonderful time with that nice young man," Mrs. T says.

"I'm sure going to try. I've got to scoot to the library to finish my paper first." She kisses Mrs. T on the cheek and starts to leave.

"By the way, I expect a full report in the morning," Mrs. T states.

Molly looks back and grins as she dashes off.

At the library, Molly rounds up some applicable references to research, sits down, opens her word processing app, and stares at a blank screen. The cursor is flashing and seems to be saying, "Come on, Come on, Come on . . ." in an annoying way. *Dr. Moore couldn't have assigned a more boring topic*, Molly thinks. Knowing that excuses and rationalizations won't cut it, she clears her mind of distractions--as much as possible--and starts to piece her paper together. As she works, her concentration improves, and her draft is completed. Molly checks her watch.

"Yipes! It's 12:42 p.m.," Molly says as she hurriedly puts her things in her backpack. She barely has time for a quick restroom stop before heading outside. One last swipe of lip gloss, and suddenly she's all thumbs. "Settle down, Molly Rae Armstrong!" she says to herself in the mirror. *Sure*, her image seems to say back to her. She bolts for the library door, speed-dialing Don on the way to tell him that she's heading for the curb. She gets his voicemail and leaves a message.

Molly's in such a rush, she doesn't even see Jackson in the crowd on the plaza in front of the library. He spots her and yells her name, but she doesn't hear him. Jackson continues to follow her through the crowd.

No vehicles are at the curb when Molly gets there; she's glad Don didn't have to wait. She wonders what kind of a vehicle Don would drive and decides it's probably an SUV of some kind--he loves the outdoors. Molly hears a fairly loud engine close by and turns in that direction. She's practically blown away by what she sees. Don drives up on a motorcycle with a sidecar--both a nice blue color--and Jasper is in the sidecar with his own little goggles on.

"Wow," she yells, "This is really cool!" She gives Jasper a pat. "And Jasper looks so handsome," Molly adds.

Jackson ducks into a crowd waiting for a bus while he continues to watch Molly. Obviously, she already knows this guy.

"Gee, thanks. What about the chauffeur?" Don says as he dismounts and unstraps a helmet on the back of the cycle.

"Well, everyone knows that you're a hunk," Molly teases with a grin.

Don smiles, hands Molly the helmet, instructs her how to put it on, and then fastens her backpack to the rear bumper of the sidecar. "I hope you don't mind, but you'll have to hold Jasper," Don states, as he picks Jasper up and sets him on the curb.

Molly replies, "Not at all--Jasper and I are becoming buddies." Don helps Molly into the sidecar and hands Jasper to her.

"Please, grab his harness on both sides and hang on," Don says while he climbs back on the motorcycle. "President Jasper and I are happy to have such a delightful passenger," Don adds, and Jasper barks.

"What did he say?" Molly coyly inquires.

"He commented that the passenger is also very pretty," Don adds.

Molly feels the warmth of a blush and leans forward to say in Jasper's ear, "You little cad!"

Don has a good laugh before he pulls out into traffic, because he knows that Molly's really referring to him. "Let's go eat and have fun," he announces.

Jackson's still standing in the crowd with a disappointed expression on his face. He's missed Molly in the last few weeks and wants to make amends, but he can't reach her. He can't find her, either--not even at school. Now it looks like she may have found someone else. Uncertain whether he'll pursue this further, he turns around and leaves.

The ride to the park is exciting and fun for Molly. It is definitely a first, and she feels like she's right down in the midst of everything--the heartbeat of the city. A feeling of intrigue sweeps over Molly, and a sense of freedom she hasn't felt for a long time.

Molly is almost on sensory overload when she looks up at Don and loudly says, "I love it!" Don smiles the biggest smile ever and even reveals some crow's feet. She is abashed by his handsomeness and practically loses her breath--a feeling she's never experienced with any man. Suddenly, she doesn't know what to feel--awe or terror. Then Molly remembers that Mrs. T told her just to be herself. *This is a new self I've never met before*, Molly thinks. And she decides tentatively to go with it--at least that's what her gut is telling her to do.

Finally they arrive at Hillcrest Greens Park--a beautiful patch of green carved out of the city with a big fountain in the middle and flower gardens on both sides. "This is beautiful, Don," Molly says. Don puts a leash on Jasper, helps Molly put her backpack on since they can't leave it, and grabs a cooler from the back of the cycle. They start to walk toward some big trees.

"I'm glad you enjoyed the ride, Molly," Don remarks.

"It filled me with a sense of belonging to my surroundings and a feeling of freedom. Oh, Mr. Jasper taught me how to enjoy the wind in my face, too," Molly says, beaming.

Don replies, "I think that's a genetic trait for dogs--the wind-loving gene."

"Sure!" Molly says with a giggle. They come to a shady spot that's relatively flat, and Don starts to set things up. He takes a Frisbee out of the cooler, and Jasper yelps. Don informs Jasper that it's for later and he stops yelping, but his semblance of a tail is going a mile a minute. Molly takes a biscuit out of her backpack and gives it to Jasper.

Don turns around with a look of disapproval and says, "Aye, methinks the wench will spoil the dog."

Molly laughs hard and gets in Don's face. "What are you going to do about it?"

Don is caught off guard by her close proximity to his lips and mutters under his breath, "Not what I'd like to do." He removes Jasper's leash and acts like he's going to whip Molly. When the fun dies down, he inquires, "How about lunch?"

"I thought ye would never ask," Molly replies. "The *wench* is hungry." They both laugh. Molly has never had a lunch like the one Don prepares. He makes chicken chutney salad and puts it in whole wheat pita pockets with fresh lettuce. He also serves a relish dish with peperoncini, Kalamata olives, and cherry tomatoes. They drink fresh-brewed iced tea and enjoy a wonderful dessert of red raspberry tarts with Chambord liqueur sauce.

"This is amazing food, Don. It has so many flavors. Thank you!" Molly says.

Don responds, "I'm glad you enjoyed it, Molly. I love to cook--it's a great outlet, and there's so much latitude for self-expression."

"My experience is limited, but I'd love to learn someday," Molly responds. "Let me clean up while you play with Jasper--he's waited long enough."

"I'll take you up on that," Don says as he picks up the Frisbee.

Molly finds a trash can and finishes cleaning up. Still savoring the tasty lunch, Molly is impressed with Don's culinary skills. She sits at the base of a tree in the shade, using the trunk as a backrest. *When was the last time I felt this contented and peaceful?* she asks herself. She enjoys watching the guys play Frisbee, and is amazed at how high that little

Jasper can jump. Finally they've had enough. Don gives Jasper some water, and they join Molly under the tree.

"President Jasper wins again, huh?" Molly chides Don.

"Please don't tell him this, but he's such a fierce competitor, I let him win," Don replies.

"Yeah, right!" Molly responds, as she hands Don some more iced tea. Don thanks Molly and asks how she's doing.

"I'm so relaxed. I'm definitely enjoying myself. And the motorcycle ride still has me very intrigued. Where did you get your cycle and sidecar?" Molly inquires.

Don tells Molly that the cycle and sidecar belonged to his father, and he inherited them when his father died five years ago. That's the first personal information Don has shared with her.

"It's so hard to lose a parent. Does your mother live close by?" Molly asks.

"No, but she lives in Providence, Rhode Island--about 200 miles away. I can be there in three and a half hours."

"That's good. I hope you get to see her often," Molly says and pauses. "I lost my mother when I was only seventeen."

Not wanting to press her for more information, Don says, "That's sad--I imagine the teenage years are a very important time in a girl's life, and she needs her mother. If she were here, I'm certain she would be very proud of you now. Do you have anyone else?"

Molly's quiet for a few seconds, and Don's afraid he's treading on thin ice. It feels like uncharted territory, but she volunteers the information about her brother, Jason. Don says he'd be happy to help Molly with her search, and she agrees that they'll discuss it the next time she's at the coffee shop.

The conversation is at a lull, and Don decides now is as good a time as any to ask Molly if she's seeing anyone else. He turns to Molly, swallows, and says, "Molly, there's something important I'd like to ask you."

"What is it?" Molly inquires, her curiosity evident.

"I've wanted to ask you for some time if you're seeing any other guy," Don answers.

Molly bristles, "There isn't another guy in the picture. Why are you asking me that?"

"Because you never let me pick you up or take you home--it's like you're hiding something," Don responds.

"What business is it of yours?" Molly retorts, jumping to her feet.

Don jumps up, too. "I didn't mean to upset you--that's the last thing I would want," he says.

Molly starts to get her things together and asks, "What do you want--to interrogate me?"

Don can't take it anymore. He reaches out and takes hold of Molly's arm, looks her in the face and says, "I care about you Molly--a lot. I want to see more of you and be a part of your life."

Their eyes are fixed on each other, and Molly's eyes are searching for answers. Don quickly but gently pulls Molly into his chest and kisses her. It's a long, passionate, breathless, sweet, hot, loving kiss like no other kiss Molly has had; she's reeling. Her legs feel like putty, and she simply melts into bliss. She's afraid to open her eyes--afraid it is all just a dream. As Molly opens her eyes, she realizes her feelings for Don are strong and knows that things will never be the same. That's what she gets for dropping her guard. The *moment of truth* is here, and it's time to find out what Don Greene is made of.

Still facing Don, she carefully says, "I don't have you pick me up or take me home because I live in a women's shelter--I recently became homeless." She intentionally watches Don's reaction, and notices that he actually looks concerned.

He asks, "What happened to you, Molly?"

She launches into her *triple whammy* story, and wonders what the outcome will be when she finishes. One thing is certain: She feels like she's getting a huge load off of her chest.

Don listens calmly, and then inquires, "And you didn't tell me this because?"

Molly responds, "Because I was afraid you would dump me." There, she said it!

"Molly, everyone has adversity in their lives at times--it helps us define ourselves and build character." Don continues, "I'm disappointed that you think I'm the type of man who would break off our friendship because you're going through difficult times. I'm a lot of things, but I'm not shallow or unfeeling."

"I'm really sorry, Don," Molly says as she looks down, clearly abashed.

There's a moment of silence before Don responds. "Apology accepted! But you're not getting off the hook that easily."

Molly looks up and asks, "What do you mean?"

"I'm crazy about you, Molly, and I'm asking for an exclusive relationship with you," Don replies. "What do you think?"

Molly feels almost defenseless as she meets Don's gaze. "I think I want another one of those kisses," she says with a smile. Jasper jumps for joy.

10

THE TEMPLE OF 'T'

Monday morning finds Molly on the proverbial cloud nine. She had Don take her home to the shelter yesterday, and she feels so much better now that things are out in the open. Molly can't wait to tell Mrs. T all about the picnic. Thinking about it makes Molly giddy all over again. *This is so out of character for me,* she thinks. Her usual serious exterior is trying to assert itself, but it won't win going up against true love. Molly finishes getting ready and leaves for Mrs. T's home.

Mrs. T is up in her chair dozing with Axel on her lap. Molly checks Mrs. T's pulse and gets her some water while she's waking up. Glad looks up at Molly, smiles and inquires, "How's my sweet Molly this morning?"

"I'm great, and I'm on cloud nine, Mrs. T," she replies.

Mrs. T swallows her pill and responds, "I can see that, Child--your feet aren't touching the ground. Sit down and tell me everything."

Molly--being a detail-oriented person--starts her story by talking about the difficulty she had concentrating on her studies yesterday. She moves into a delightful account of her ride in Don's sidecar with Jasper on her lap. Mrs. T is totally engrossed in Molly's new experience, especially hearing about the fabulous picnic Don prepared. Glad loves to talk about cooking and food. Then Molly launches into the boys' Frisbee toss and how high Jasper can jump. They both start to giggle over that. Molly is filled with joy watching Mrs. T laugh, and she realizes how lucky she is to have her as a friend. Mrs. T urges her on with her story.

"Everything was like a dream until we started to argue," Molly recalls.

"What about?" Mrs. T asks. "He didn't get fresh with you, did he?"

"No, Mrs. T, he's a perfect gentleman," Molly relates. "He blatantly asked me if I'm seeing another man. I don't blame him--I've always gone to the coffee shop to see him. I wouldn't let him take me home or pick me up at the shelter. And yesterday I had him pick me up at the library. I was afraid I would lose him if he found out I'm homeless."

"Oh, Child, he must have become suspicious," Mrs. T comments.

"At first I had a typical juvenile reaction and got miffed," Molly continues. "But," she adds, "It didn't stop Don from advancing his agenda."

"What do you mean?" Mrs. T asks.

"Don believed he deserved an explanation. So I gave him one." Molly takes a drink of water and continues. "I told him everything. I decided that if he dumped me because I'm homeless, he's not worth it."

Mrs. T queries, "How did Don react to that news?"

"I got a surprise reaction," Molly says. "Don got upset with me because I didn't confide in him and tell him the truth. Actually, he was very concerned about me."

"I told you he's a good guy--I just feel it in my gut. What happened?" Mrs. T inquires.

"We were at an impasse; he pulled me into his arms and gave me a long, passionate kiss," Molly responds. "Boy that changed the scenario. Suddenly I realized how strong my feelings are for him, and I apologized for not confiding in him."

"He accepted your apology, right?" Mrs. T asks.

"He accepted my apology, informed me that he's crazy about me and asked for an exclusive relationship," Molly says with a big smile. "I moved in for another one of those kisses."

Mrs. T laughs and slaps her leg with her hand. "This sounds like a *happily ever after* story to me. I'm full of joy and excitement for you, Molly--you deserve it!"

"Thank you, Mrs. T. Somehow I feel whole and centered now. And, I hate to do this, but I've got to run to class." Molly gets up and kisses Mrs. T. "I'm so happy I have you in my life, Mrs. T--you're truly special," she says.

"I love you, Child," Mrs. T replies, "and I think you're precious."

Molly yells over her shoulder, "I'll make lunch if I can."

❧

It's another beautiful day--unseasonably warm, but starting to cool down, Molly notes as she walks to school. Her cell phone rings and the display shows Don's name. She smiles sweetly and answers with, "Good morning, Don."

"Well, I called to say good morning to you. Where are you?" Don asks.

"About two blocks from school; I have a 10:00 a.m. class," Molly responds, "and then I may have lunch with Mrs. T."

"OK, I'm just checking in and thinking about you." Don says.

"Oh, I'm thinking about you and Mr. Jasper, too," Molly declares. "I'll call you later so we can touch bases." They say their goodbyes. Molly picks up her pace to get to class on time and turn in that ridiculous paper about budgets.

❧

After class, Molly heads for Hunger's Kitchen to grab lunch with Mrs. T. One thing that's amazing about Mrs. T is that she arrives at Hunger's Kitchen everyday at the same time. Molly doesn't know how she does it--Mrs. T doesn't wear a watch. When Molly gets to the Kitchen, Mrs. T isn't in line. She peeks inside the building, too, and starts asking people if they've seen her. One lady who knows Mrs. T informs Molly that Glad didn't show up today. Concerned, Molly takes off for Mrs. T's box. It isn't like her to miss lunch. She hopes nothing has happened to Axel, either.

When Molly arrives at Mrs. T's box, she doesn't immediately see her or Axel. She finds Mrs. T curled up in the box, with Axel right next to her. *She must have fallen asleep,* Molly thinks, and gets down on her knees to check on her. But Mrs. T doesn't stir. Axle meows softly--like he's trying to tell Molly something. She crawls into the box to check Mrs. T's pulse--but she doesn't feel a pulse. Molly puts her ear to Mrs. T's chest and doesn't hear a heartbeat or respirations, and her body is cool to the touch. A gut-wrenching, shrill, "No, Mrs. T," erupts from deep within Molly's soul, and she starts to sob uncontrollably. She holds Mrs. T's body with one hand and strokes Axel with the other.

A few homeless people start to gather around the box to coax Molly out. Still crying, Molly tries to comfort Glad's friends. No one witnessed anyone unusual hanging around. They believe Mrs. T just slipped away in her sleep. Molly sits down in Mrs. T's chair and dials 911 to report what has happened. Then she calls Lucy to ask if she'll allow her to bring Axel to the shelter. Lucy isn't too keen on cats, but can't say no to Molly, who's totally distraught.

After all, Axel is all Molly has left of Mrs. T. She does her best to console Molly over the phone.

"I'm so sorry that Mrs. T is gone, Molly--she was like a grandmother to you. Do you want me to come over there and help?" Lucy asks.

"That's so kind of you to offer, Lucy, but I'm going to call Don. He has a carrier that we can use to transport Axel to the shelter," Molly responds. "May I put him on the back patio?"

"Sure, Molly, that will be fine. I'll put a bowl of water out there," Lucy replies.

The two ladies say their goodbyes, and Molly gets more facial tissue out of her backpack. She's a little more collected now, so she calls Don. When he answers, Molly starts telling him about Mrs. T's death, and she starts to cry again. She relates how she found Mrs. T's body with Axel curled up next to her--like they were napping.

"Oh, Molly, I'm so sorry to hear that you've lost your good friend. Let me find someone to cover the shop for me so I can come over there to be with you and help," Don offers.

"I would love that, Don. Would you help me take Axel to Alma de Lucy? Lucy said he can stay there."

"Of course I will, Honey. I'll bring a carrier. Let me start making some calls, and when I get someone to cover, I'll call you back for directions," Don says.

Molly responds, "Oh, Don, I appreciate this so much. Mrs. T always told me that you're a good guy--she felt it in her gut." They say goodbye and after she hangs up, she realizes that Don called her *Honey* for the first time. "Mrs. T was right," she mutters to herself.

Two policemen show up to investigate Mrs. T's death. They tell Molly that the medical examiner (ME) will be there soon. Molly explains how she found Mrs. T, and also tells them that she's taking the cat to her home. They inquire about where she lives, and she tells them the truth--Alma de Lucy.

"Sure," one officer says. "What's going to happen to the cat at the end of your thirty days?"

Molly informs them that she's Lucy Mercado's assistant manager and lives there permanently. She offers to call Lucy to confirm that information.

"No, we believe you," the officers' reply. "But please have the cat neutered."

Molly agrees and thinks how much she hates the business side of things--she just lost her best friend. Don calls her back and she gives him directions to Mrs. T's house. She informs him that the police are there and that the ME is on his way.

"I'll be right over," Don says.

The ME finally arrives and Molly makes sure that the policemen relate the facts correctly. Molly tells the ME that Mrs. T just turned 78, had congestive heart failure and was under the care of Dr. Rollin Clark at the free clinic. She tells them that she checked Mrs. T's pulse every morning before she took her medicine, and she gives the remaining digitalis tablets to the ME. The ME starts to examine Mrs. T's body.

Don arrives and Molly puts Axel in the carrier right away. Don holds her while the ME concludes his exam, and Mrs. T's body is loaded into an ambulance. Molly starts to cry again as the ambulance drives away.

Finally the ME advises the policemen and Molly that there doesn't appear to be any foul play--she probably died of natural causes between 10:30 to 11:30 a.m. He says that her body will be taken to the city morgue for an autopsy before he releases a final report. Molly indicates that she's the local contact and will be arranging a memorial service for Mrs. T.

The ME inquires of Molly, "Are you a family member?"

"No," Molly responds. "I regarded her as my surrogate grandmother, though."

"In a legal capacity?" the ME presses.

"No," Molly responds, and that's the end of their conversation.

The ME goes into his *business as usual* mode and advises everyone that "Our office will hold the body for up to four weeks--pending notification of any family we're able to identify. We will only release her body to mortuary officials," the ME says matter-of-factly.

"He sounds like a recording," Molly whispers in Don's ear. Don pats her on the back in acknowledgment. The ME packs up his equipment and leaves.

The police start to collect all of Mrs. T's personal effects to hold as potential evidence, pending release of the final ME's report, presumably attributing the death to natural causes.

Molly intervenes with, "You have a preliminary report. Please let me have one blanket for Axel's bed--he was her soul mate." The tears start to roll down her cheeks again, and she pleads, "Please!"

The two policemen look at each other, and Molly gets a brief glimpse of their humanitarian sides. The younger policeman looks at his partner and asks, "Don't you think we could let her have one small blanket?" The partner hesitates, but makes the mistake of looking at Molly.

"Sure," he replies. "But this didn't happen, OK?"

Molly answers with, "You have my word." He motions her to the box, where Molly selects a small blanket and holds it to her chest.

"Thank you so much, officers," she says. They finish gathering Mrs. T's belongings and leave. Only the empty cardboard box is left.

Don tries to comfort Molly and asks, "What else can I do to help you, Molly?"

"I've decided to leave Mrs. T's box as a memorial," Molly states. "Then we can go to the shelter." Molly hands Don the blanket and takes a black marker from her backpack. She kneels on the sidewalk and writes on the box, *Gladys Mae Teaberry, November 5th, 2014. Rest in Peace, Sweet Angel.*

Without making eye contact with Don, Molly says, "What kind of a world allows people to die in cardboard boxes? If I had the money, I'd erect a temple for Mrs. T." She then sits down on the curb to collect herself. Don sits next to her on the curb and hands her Mrs. T's blanket, which Molly holds to her chest and caresses.

"Let's go, Honey!" Don gently urges. "Let's take Axel to his new home." He stands up and puts out his hand for Molly. She gets up from the curb, and Don gently hugs her one more time before he picks up Axel's carrier. They silently walk to Alma de Lucy, making a quick stop at the discount store for Don to buy dry cat food, a bowl, a litter box, and litter.

Don is allowed to walk through the shelter to carry Axel to the back patio.

"May I keep the carrier for a while to use it as Axel's house?" Molly asks.

"Sure, Molly. It's a little small for Jasper, anyway." Don sets Axel's carrier up against the shelter wall, next to the heat vent. The water bowl is on the patio, as Lucy promised, and Molly places the food bowl next to it. She sits down on the patio next to the carrier and opens the door. Axel spots the water and food bowls and sniffs around them. Molly strokes his fur, and he turns to face her and sits down.

"Your mama is gone now, Axel, and this is your new home," Molly says sadly. She offers Mrs. T's blanket for him to smell.

"Don't worry, I'll love and take care of you always," Molly continues.

She's about to shake the blanket out to fold it for the carrier, and stops. Feeling the blanket, she says to Don,

"There's something hard in here." She gently unfolds the blanket and finds the earrings she gave Mrs. T for her birthday. She picks them up, holds them to her heart and gently starts to cry again. Don sits down to comfort Molly and look at the earrings.

Molly looks up at the sky and says, "I'll cherish these earrings always, Mrs. T, but the best gift you've given me is a portion of yourself. For that I'm both honored and blessed." She puts the earrings in her pocket, folds the blanket, and puts it in Axel's carrier.

After Don leaves, Molly appears in the dining room and is greeted with warm hugs and condolences. Grateful, she thanks Lucy and the guests. Molly only eats a few bites of mashed potatoes and gravy and excuses herself to go to bed. She's able to doze off and on but keeps reviewing the horrendous events of the day over and over--like a bad video tape playing in her head.

In the middle of the night, Molly hears Axel meowing at the back door. She tiptoes into the dining room, opens the patio door and picks Axel up. Molly quietly carries him to her bed, puts him under the covers, and he snuggles up next to her. Totally exhausted, they finally settle down for a restful sleep together.

11

TRUST

Mrs. T's death plunges Molly into the depths of loneliness, and not even Don can reach her. He's there for her when she needs him--even if he just sits quietly by her side. Occasionally she talks, but not to make conversation. She verbalizes all of her regrets about Mrs. T--especially the fact that Don didn't get to meet her.

Out of love and respect, Don allows Molly the alone time she needs to work through the grief process. When his father died, Don discovered that grief is personal and different for each individual. Don's heart aches because Molly's heart is aching, but hers will heal at its own rate. Molly's like a wounded bird--give her shelter until she heals.

Axel is slowly adjusting to his new home. Lucy observes how good he is for morale and is starting to come around. In fact, Axel's becoming quite the lady's man. Several of the guests adore him, pet him, play with him and sneak him tidbits from the table. Molly would admonish them, but she does the same thing. Mrs. T said he's five years old, so at this time in his life, he's still quite athletic. Molly keeps an eye on Axel's weight, just in case.

Lucy and Don keep a close eye on Molly, especially Lucy, as she's in a position to ensure that Molly's getting adequate nutrition and rest. Molly continues to do all of the chores she's been given, and even though she broods less when she's busy, Lucy can tell that Molly's heart just isn't involved yet.

Molly calls the coroner's office almost every day. When she tries to seek information about Mrs. T's death certificate, she is asked whether she's a blood relative. When she responds "No," she is informed that the only way she can get a copy is to present documentation showing entitlement, i.e., an insurance policy, will, bank book or statement, or property deed. The officials tell her they're still trying to locate Mrs. T's family. Molly, discouraged, is glum for most of the day.

It's amazing, but Molly hasn't missed any classes--in spite of her grief. She stops by Mrs. T's cardboard box every day. The box has indeed become a temple for Mrs. T, and it now leans a little to one side because of the weight. People have placed flowers; plants; little gifts like a tiny toy cat; and lots of handwritten notes, poetry and signs on and around the box. Molly takes time to read everything. Most of the notes say thank you for some kind, considerate act Mrs. T had performed for a soul in need. Molly is touched, considering that besides her own mother; Mrs. T was the most compassionate, loving person in her life.

That afternoon, Molly gets a call from Rudy. "How are you holding up, my dear friend?" he asks kindly.

"I'm holding my own--barely. There's so much that needs to be done, and my hands are tied by the coroner's office because I don't have any personal information on Mrs. T," Molly laments.

Rudy interjects, "Well, she's got to have family some-where that can help."

"The coroner's office is working on that right now. I'll just have to wait," she replies.

"There's something I need to tell you about. The ru-mor on the street is there's a very proper-looking gentle-man searching for you," Rudy reports. "Apparently, he goes by Mrs. T's box every day and asks the locals about you."

Molly's interest is piqued. "I wonder who he could be. I hope I'm not in any trouble."

"The locals report that he's usually there around 10:00 a.m. every day and he's polite, but businesslike. Perhaps you can find him there tomorrow and determine what he's looking for. Do you want me to be there?" Rudy asks.

"Thanks for offering, Rudy, but I need to do this on my own. There are always people around," Molly says. "Stop worrying so much, OK?"

"OK, Molly, but you call me if you need me, and I'll be right there."

Molly thinks, *I'm sure he will--he's so protective. He'll probably hide in the box.* She thanks Rudy again and they say their goodbyes.

The next morning, Molly skips class and is at Mrs. T's box by 9:45 a.m. She looks over all of the gifts and starts to read the new notes. Every expression of loss is so heartfelt and genuine--*this is truly a special place*, Molly thinks.

"Excuse me!" a male voice says from behind Molly's back, "Are you Molly Rae Armstrong?"

She turns to face the man while responding, "Yes, I am. What may I do for you?" He is a well-dressed, nice-looking, middle-aged man of medium build with graying temples and hazel eyes. He hands Molly a business card and introduces himself as Max Burnett, attorney at law.

"I'd like to talk with you about Gladys Mae Teaberry. Do you have a few minutes?" he inquires.

"Sure, Mr. Burnett, anything I can do to help," Molly replies.

Max looks around until he sees a coffee shop, and turns to Molly to ask, "Would you be kind enough to join me for a cup of coffee so we can sit down for a few minutes?"

"OK," Molly says, and the two of them head for the coffee shop together.

Mr. Burnett says, "Gladys Teaberry was such a lovely lady, I'm truly saddened by her passing."

Molly's eyes get a little moist, so she doesn't look up when she responds: "She was like a grandmother to me and was a very precious person."

Mr. Burnett opens the café door for Molly, and they enter. The café is old, but clean, and is about half full. He guides Molly to a booth in the back corner.

"May I call you Molly?" Mr. Burnett asks, and Molly nods. The waitress comes to take their orders.

"Mrs. Teaberry came to me about one month ago to draw up and execute a new trust and last will and testament. She did love you like a granddaughter, Molly, and wanted to make a bequest for you." Molly's eyes widen as she raises her eyebrows in surprise, and Mr. Burnett pauses.

"Before I proceed, would you be kind enough to show me some identification?"

Molly gets her wallet out and produces her driver's license and school ID.

"You may not have known this about Mrs. Teaberry, but she was once a wealthy socialite in Louisiana. She had two sons who continuously bickered over her money; she became so upset and disillusioned that she left home and became disenfranchised. I'm her trustee and have managed her trust for eight years," Mr. Burnett states.

"Mrs. T only spoke of her past one time," Molly relates, "and that was to tell me a story about her mother."

"Mrs. Teaberry spoke to me about you, Molly. She said you were very protective of her and your love was true--like the love of a small, innocent child. Gladys believed in you and wants you to finish school and succeed." Mr. Burnett pulls an envelope out of his coat, takes the contents out and unfolds the papers. He turns the papers around so Molly can read them and points to one line.

"Molly, Mrs. Teaberry left you a bequest of 2.5 million dollars," Mr. Burnett advises.

Molly gasps and starts to cry. She suddenly feels numb and doesn't know how to react. She looks at the trust and there it is, "Molly Rae Armstrong, $2,500,000.00."

Mr. Burnett motions for the waitress to bring Molly some water. Molly takes a few sips, but is still stunned. Finally, she inquires, "What about her family? I hope they're taken care of."

"She made bequests to her two children and has created a college fund for each of her three grandchildren," Mr. Burnett responds. "They're taken care of, Molly."

Then Molly begins to discuss the difficulties she's having with the coroner's office. Mr. Burnett informs her that he'll provide her with all of the required documentation, and that burial costs will no longer be an issue. Molly breathes a sigh of relief. She can now arrange a beautiful service for Mrs. T--like she deserves.

Mr. Burnett inquires, "Are you available to meet with me at my office on Thursday--say, 2:00 p.m.? We can go over everything then, take care of the paperwork, and get you the documentation you need to prove entitlement."

"Yes, I'll be there, and I'll need some additional assistance from you," Molly states.

"How may I help you, Molly?" Mr. Burnett inquires.

"I'll need your expertise to establish The Gladys Mae Teaberry Charitable Foundation," Molly says. "She had a real passion and love for homeless people and can now make a measurable difference. Will you help?"

"I'll gladly assist in any way I can, Molly," he replies. They both rise, and he reconfirms their appointment on Thursday.

They shake hands as Molly says, "Thank you, Mr. Burnett. I'll be a deserving recipient."

"I know you will, Molly," Mr. Burnett says as he heads for the door. He turns back to say, "By the way, you may call me Max." He leaves the shop, and Molly sits down again.

This is unbelievable, Molly thinks. *I still need to get hold of myself.* She folds up Mrs. T's trust and puts it in her backpack. *Don is going to be blown away,* she reflects. Molly remains seated for another ten minutes and sips some more water before she gets up to leave for Bean Too Long.

Suddenly, she feels the need for one of Don's generous, warm hugs.

When Molly gets to the coffee house, Don has two customers and is working behind the counter. He looks up when Molly enters and displays a warm smile. By the time Molly reaches the counter, Don has dried his hands and offers her a tender hug, which is well reciprocated--she even throws in a kiss on his cheek. By this time, Jasper is at Molly's feet making his little yelping sounds, and she smiles as she bends down to pet him.

"How lucky can I get? Both guys are happy to see me," Molly says with a smile, as she slips Jasper a biscuit.

"Happy? Jubilant is more like it," Don remarks, "How did you know we're missing you?"

"Mostly because I'm missing you, too," she replies.

Suddenly the door opens and six people come in. "Oh, boy!" Don says under his breath.

Molly goes behind the counter and puts on an apron. "I want to help. What may I do?"

"OK," Don responds, "You take care of the food part of the orders and I'll fix the drinks." Don steps up to the counter to take orders; Molly grabs a pen and a pad of paper and takes the next person in line. They're filling the orders in no time, and Molly only has to ask one question. About the time all of the orders are ready, the other two people leave, and Molly cleans the table.

While putting things back in order behind the counter, Don exclaims, "We make a great team, Molly Armstrong."

"So it seems," Molly responds.

"I don't have a class tonight. How about going to my place when Ben gets here to work the p.m. shift? He should be here in the next twenty minutes," Don comments. "I'll cook you some dinner and we can get caught up" Don proposes, putting his hands together as though he's praying.

"You don't have to be so melodramatic, Mister!" Molly says teasingly. "It sounds like a good plan to me."

Don is pleased, and he's especially happy to see that Molly's personality is returning. "Great!" he says, kissing her on the cheek.

"Let me go call Lucy and let her know. She'll get concerned if I don't show up for supper," Molly says as she walks out the front door with her phone.

Shortly before 2:00 p.m., Ben Moto arrives to work his shift. Don introduces Ben to Molly before they leave. The three of them exchange some pleasantries and Don, Molly, and Jasper go out the back door, where the cycle is parked. Don hands Molly a helmet and says, "Here, you know the drill." Molly smiles as she dons her helmet, and Jasper starts jumping with excitement.

They have a nice, quiet ride to Don's apartment, which isn't too far away. Don lives in an older neighborhood with tall trees and old, well-kept apartment buildings. The leaves are turning brilliant shades, and Molly takes a deep breath to smell the scents of autumn. Once inside the building, Don shows Molly around his one-bedroom apartment. Molly notes that the apartment is very nicely decorated, inviting, and appears comfortable and clean.

"It wasn't easy to find a place in this area where pets are allowed. Another plus is the laundry room on the main floor," Don comments. He motions toward the couch and says, "Have a seat, and I'll get us some cold drinks." He flips on a CD player, and Nora Jones starts to sing. Molly enjoys the music, closes her eyes, and feels like she's in a good place where she belongs. She doesn't know when she'll tell Don that she's a millionaire, but *no time like the present*, she thinks.

Don sits down on the couch with a couple of lemonades and hands one to Molly. She then surprises him by asking about his plans for the second floor of the coffee shop building.

"I'd love to turn it into a two-bedroom apartment," Don replies.

"Would there be any office space in the apartment?" Molly inquires.

Don answers, "There could be. Now I'm really intrigued by your questions. Why are you asking?"

"Well, I'm wondering if you'll lease the space to me to use as an office," Molly says.

Don sits up on the edge of the couch. "Molly," he says, "did you find some incredible job?"

"Yes," Molly replies as she reaches for her backpack. She takes out the trust paperwork and tells Don, "Mrs. T left me a gift." She shows Don the paperwork and points to the $2.5 million line.

Don's eyes get really wide, and he jumps up. "Holy guacamole," he practically shouts. "My girlfriend's a millionaire." More quietly, he jibes, "Will she still have a pauper barista like me?"

Molly pats the couch for him to sit back down. "Of course I'll hang on to my *pauper barista*. He's just the guy to help me realize my new dream as the trustee of The Gladys Mae Teaberry Charitable Foundation."

"That's incredible, Molly. Congratulations!" Don responds. "There's no one else in the world but you for this position. How did all of this come about?"

Molly relates the events of the day to Don--meeting Max Burnett, having coffee, talking about Mrs. T and her family, and Max informing her about the bequest. "I felt so weird, I got light-headed and thought I was going to pass out," Molly says.

"What happened to you?" Don asks.

"I sipped some water and sat another ten minutes after Max left. I'm OK now."

"Good, Honey!" Don puts his arm around Molly and holds her. They continue to talk for a good hour about the foundation, Molly's vision, and implementation plans.

"How about we continue our conversation over dinner?" Molly finally suggests.

"You're hungry? This is good. Let's get to work," Don replies. They go into the kitchen to prepare dinner and talk nonstop. Molly tells Don she has an appointment with Max on Thursday. She explains how relieved she is that she'll have the documentation she needs for the coroner's office. And with burial costs taken care of, she'll be able to have a beautiful memorial service for Mrs. T. *I'd better start planning her service now*, Molly thinks.

After a delicious dinner and cleanup, Don and Molly's shoes are off and they end up back on the couch, cuddling.

"There's one thing we haven't discussed, and it's coming up real soon," Don says.

"What's that--Thanksgiving?" Molly inquires.

"Yes, I'll be going to Rhode Island to have Thanksgiving dinner with my mother and a few other relatives. I'd love for you to meet my family--will you be able to go?"

"I wish I could. I'm sure it will be wonderful, but I'm already committed to help Lucy with dinner for the Alma de Lucy guests. Sorry, Honey!"

"I'm sorry you can't go, too. A little getaway would be nice," Don observes. "But, we'll have other opportunities in the future."

They talk some more, and Molly drifts into a restful sleep. Not wanting to disturb her, Don gets up carefully, puts a pillow under Molly's head, pulls her legs up, and covers her with an afghan. He grabs another afghan and takes a big chair across from her--he wants to be near her. Jasper jumps up on the couch and settles down by Molly's feet. Don gazes at her fondly and says in a soft voice, "I truly love you, Molly Rae Armstrong. It doesn't matter to me if you're a millionaire or a bag lady--you're the woman for me."

12

GRANDDAUGHTERS

The day is overcast, and Molly busies herself completing the paperwork for the coroner's office. She's already been to the department store to buy an attractive outfit for Mrs. T. Suddenly; she's been thrust into the role of a businesswoman, while maintaining her status as a full-time student and Lucy's assistant manager. She's clearly overloaded. Lucy is aware of this and limits Molly's duties as much as she can.

Sometimes Molly takes a breather. More often, however, she uses her down time to think about everything that needs to be done. She has to have Mrs. T's body transferred to the mortuary, deliver her clothing and arrange for her burial and memorial service. She also has to create the foundation with Max and study for mid-term exams. As if that weren't enough, Thanksgiving will be here in a week, and she'll be helping Lucy with preparations.

Oh, and incidentally, her twenty-fifth birthday will be December 6th.

Molly's meeting with Max Burnett is today, and his office is far enough away that she takes a taxi. The taxi stops at a beautiful art deco office building. Molly takes the elevator up to the twelfth floor. The receptionist greets her with a smile. "You must be Molly," she says. "Would you like something to drink?"

When Molly declines, the receptionist says, "Please take a seat. Mr. Burnett will be right with you." The office is tastefully decorated with old oak furniture, original artwork, and lots of plants. Within five minutes, Max opens his office door and cordially invites Molly in.

Once the greeting process is completed, Max gives Molly a packet of entitlement papers, which she can use to claim Mrs. T's body. Then he begins to explain the particulars required to establish Mrs. T's foundation, and how it will work. Mrs. T graciously took care of Max's fees in advance, and when the foundation is up and running, Molly will be able to take a salary as trustee, Max explains. He picks up an envelope lying on his desk, extends it toward Molly, and says "I hope you don't mind Molly, but I've secured an advance of $750.00 to cover any current expenses you may have."

Molly's eyes get teary as she takes the envelope. "This is greatly appreciated. Thank you, Max." She puts the envelope in her purse. *I'll stop at the bank and put this in my depleted savings account on the way home,* Molly thinks.

Max is both pleasant and competent, and Molly feels comfortable with him--a good thing, she reflects, since there's a lot of complexity involved in this process. "Molly," he says, "I want you to take the paperwork home and read it. Write down any questions you might have, and we'll sit down in a week to discuss it. Then I'll answer any questions you have, and begin the start-up process. Does that suit you?"

"Yes, that's fine," Molly says. She's pleased that Max is skillful at translating from *legalese* to plain *English*.

While Max gathers up and organizes the paperwork for Molly, she looks directly at him and says, "You may or may not be aware of this, but I've been homeless for several months."

He nods and replies, "I suspected that was the case, from the difficulty I had in finding you. I must say, you look very well for living on the streets."

"Oh, I got lucky and found a women's shelter the first night," Molly responds. "But the irony of the situation is that I never would have met Glad if the course of my life hadn't changed to adversity." Her eyes get teary as she looks down and continues, "This has been a lot more than a character-building exercise for me. I'm actually very humbled and grateful."

"Gladys recognized those qualities in you, Molly--I think she saw a little of herself in you," Max relates.

Molly looks up at Max and replies, "And I saw the woman I'd like to be someday, thanks to Glad. I was a fearful, vulnerable girl at first, but Glad taught me about life and existence. Because of her love and encouragement, I'm developing wisdom and toughness."

Max interjects, "You had a great mentor, Molly. Glad watched you grow, and she was proud of you."

He hands Molly a file, and she stands up. "Thank you, Max. Glad was an amazing woman. And the biggest lesson she taught me was that adversity really isn't a curse; it's a big challenge--but it's also an opportunity."

"Glad was right; you'll do well in this position. I can understand why she was so proud," Max remarks. He smiles warmly at Molly, shakes her hand, and advises her to make her return appointment on the way out. Molly is smiling as she leaves his office.

Coincidentally, Don's minding the coffee shop, studying for his mid-terms, working on a paper, and is beginning to interview architects for the upstairs renovation. He and Molly are enthusiastic about the remodeling project, and there's ample space for a nice office within the apartment.

Molly confided in Lucy about the new trustee position in her life, and Lucy's incredibly excited. She's glad that Molly will stay at Alma de Lucy until Don's space is remodeled--a project that may take three to four months. This will give Lucy ample time to select Molly's replacement, although she hates to see Molly go--she's grown so fond of her *little sister*. Molly assures Lucy, however, that she will need her expertise to determine the most meaningful programs and interventions for the homeless. "This isn't goodbye," Molly tells Lucy. "You'll have a voice in the foundation, and we'll see each other regularly."

The peace of the afternoon is interrupted when Molly's cell phone rings. The display shows area code *607*. Molly doesn't know where that is, but she answers with "Hello."

"May I please speak with Molly Armstrong?" a female voice requests.

"This is Molly. How may I help you?" she inquires.

There's a slight pause on the line. "Molly, this is Lauren Teaberry. The coroner's office gave me your name and number as a contact for my grandmother's estate."

This could get awkward, Molly thinks. "Yes, Glad was a very dear friend of mine."

Lauren inquires further, "Are you arranging her funeral service?"

"Yes," Molly responds. "I'm finishing the paperwork for the coroner right now. Then her body will be released to the mortuary." The woman sounds kind, and Molly decides to go out on a limb. "Would you like to help with her service? Having a family member involved would be so meaningful."

"I'd love to help with the service, Molly--I adored my *Grandma Glad*. Can you meet with me this Saturday?" Lauren asks.

"Sure, where are you located?" Molly inquires.

"Ithaca," Lauren says. "I go to Cornell and can drive down on Saturday morning."

"That's great, Lauren. We'll have an early lunch and plan Glad's service," Molly suggests.

"I'll plan to arrive between 11:00 and 11:30 a.m., then. Where will I meet you?"

Molly gives her the address of Bean Too Long. Privacy is at a premium at the shelter, and Lauren probably doesn't know she's been homeless--not that it matters anymore. The two women agree on the meeting, and neither detects the other's nervousness. *I wonder what lies in store*, Molly thinks. She calls Don to tell him the news.

The next day, Molly goes to The Office of Chief Medical Examiner to submit the paperwork that will release Mrs. T's body to the mortuary. In turn, Molly receives Mrs. T's personal effects, sealed in a plastic bag. Now that Lauren's in the picture, Molly wouldn't feel right going through the contents of the bag by herself. She decides to save it for Saturday, and she and Lauren can open it together.

Saturday morning arrives, and Molly anxiously awaits Lauren's arrival at Bean Too Long. All kinds of scenarios are playing in her head, but she tries to focus on the positive ones. Finally, at 11:15 a.m., a petite woman with blond hair--around the age of 21--walks through the door. Not only is she beautiful, she has twinkly blue eyes. Molly knows this is Lauren, so she stands up and extends her hand. If Molly had to describe Lauren's demeanor, she would characterize her as cultured and confident.

"I'm so pleased you could come," Molly says. She introduces Lauren to Don, and he advises them that lunch is almost ready. Of course Jasper comes out of the back room to check out the new visitor. He sits at Molly's feet, and she slips him a biscuit. Molly and Lauren sit down and, as an ice breaker, trade information about their schools.

"What do you major in at Cornell, Lauren?" Molly inquires.

"I'm majoring in human development in the College of Human Ecology."

Molly prods further. "What's your concentration?"

"Law, psychology and human development," Lauren replies, "Not too many people ask me that."

Wow, Molly thinks, *with those credentials, Lauren could assist the homeless immensely. She'd be perfect for a position at the foundation, hopefully as a board member.* Molly makes a mental note. Don brings their lunch to the table, and they invite him to join them as they continue getting acquainted.

"I'd know you anywhere, Lauren," Molly states. "You have your grandmother's eyes."

Lauren smiles and responds, "Hopefully, I also have her heart, fortitude, and her moxie."

"She was an amazing woman, whom I was privileged to know," Molly observes. Thus begins their conversation about Glad and her life. Molly is fascinated to hear Lauren relate personal stories about Glad. When they finish their lunch, Don clears the table, and Molly laments, "I hate talking about Glad in the past tense. She encouraged me and helped me grow. I truly loved her, Lauren."

"I'm glad she had someone to care for her and help her, Molly," Lauren says warmly. "You may have been her only source of emotional support." Lauren was aware that Glad was living on the street, but didn't know where--Glad completely dropped out of society. She got a few letters from her grandmother, but they were all mailed from different states. Friends who were transient must have mailed them while on the road.

"That saddens me," Molly responds, "but she had a lot of friends here, and everyone thought highly of her."

"That's comforting to know," Lauren says. "My father and uncle are so obsessed with money, that their greed drove *Grandma Glad* away."

"That must have been painfully difficult for you to watch," Molly replies.

Lauren's eyes tear. "Yes, and it created a wedge between me and my father." Then Lauren relates how she felt when her father called to tell her about Glad's death. "*Grandma*

Glad lovingly supported her sons, and they won't even attend her funeral." Lauren's primary emotion was sadness, but there was an underlying sense of anger--not at Glad, but at circumstances. "If only I had known that *Grandma Glad* was in Brooklyn! I could have visited her and helped her. This is such a tragedy," Lauren cries.

Molly tells Lauren about Glad's life on the streets; about her soul mate, Axel; and her health issues. Feeling that this would be a good time to go through Glad's personal effects, she plucks the bag off the chair next to her and puts it on the table between the two of them. "Lauren, these are Glad's things. I got them from the coroner's office. I haven't opened it--I wanted to wait until you were here."

Lauren takes the bag and opens it, but there isn't much to go through. Lauren picks up a beautiful gold locket and opens it to see a picture of her great-grandparents. There are four tattered photographs, including one of Glad and her husband, Glad's two sons, all of the grandchildren, and a wonderful picture of Lauren when she was around the age of ten years. Lauren gets tears in her eyes as she shows and explains each item to Molly. Then she pulls Molly's birthday card and unused candle out of the bag. She asks Molly for permission to read the card.

"Of course," says Molly.

"This is wonderfully touching, Molly," Lauren says after she finishes reading. "I can tell it was written from the heart, and I'm so glad my grandma had someone to love and be loved by in return before she passed."

Tears begin to roll down Molly's cheeks, and she and Lauren both reach for napkins on the table. Molly asks Lauren if she may keep the card and the candle, and Lauren nods. They decide they had better get Glad's memorial service planned, as Lauren has to leave around 2:00 p.m. to drive back to Ithaca. To begin with, they set the date for two weeks away--after mid-term exams and Thanksgiving.

"What are you thinking about for the service, Molly?" Lauren inquires.

"I'm thinking about having a graveside service only, with refreshments served afterward. Most of Glad's friends aren't very mobile, and I feel it would be best for them to only have one location to go to," Molly says. She tells Lauren about the lovely clothing she purchased for Glad, and shows her a picture of the gravestone she's selected. It has a tall statue of an angel, with roses at her feet. Lauren admires the headstone. "*Grandma Glad* would be very pleased--roses were her favorite flower," Lauren says.

"Lauren," Molly inquires, "would you please call the company and advise them what to inscribe on Glad's gravestone?"

"Certainly, Molly. I'd be glad to do that. Thank you for asking," she adds.

"Is there a religious preference for the service?" Molly inquires, and Lauren advises her that a Protestant minister will be fine. They decide the clergyperson can begin with a blessing, and Lauren and Molly will both deliver short eulogies before the benediction.

"Can you think of anything else?" Molly inquires.

"Not right this moment, Molly. You seem to have thought of everything, and I like what you've done. Thank you, so much."

Things are obviously starting to wind down, and Lauren hasn't asked anything about her grandmother's bequest to Molly.

"There's one more thing I'd like to tell you, Lauren," Molly says. Lauren leans forward. "You're grandmother's estate is being rolled into a foundation--The Gladys Mae Teaberry Charitable Foundation. She was so passionate about homeless and disenfranchised people--their cause and their plight. Everything she did for them was done with love, kindness, consideration and respect." Lauren nods as Molly continues. "The foundation will truly make a difference and impact lives for the better by offering services like counseling, training classes, assistance with housing, food, child care, and clothing. An analysis will be performed to identify the most significant needs of this population and any gaps that Medicaid doesn't cover," Molly says, her enthusiasm infectious as she warms to her topic.

"This sounds huge, Molly, but I can see your drive and passion for the cause," Lauren comments. "I believe that *Grandma Glad* would be very pleased with your plan."

"Thanks for your vote of confidence, Lauren. That means a lot to me, and I'd like to talk with you more about this in the future," Molly says, handing Lauren the bag with Mrs. T's personal effects.

"Absolutely, the foundation sounds incredible." In fact, Lauren is blown away by the scope of Molly's plan. She is certain her grandmother visualized great things for Molly. She tells Molly she'll call in a couple of days to touch bases about *Grandma Glad's* service. The two shake hands warmly, and Lauren leaves for Ithaca.

Over the course of the next two weeks, Lauren and Molly talk several times to ensure that all of the details for Glad's service are taken care of. When time permits, they talk about other things, and a friendship begins to form and build.

The mortuary helped Molly obtain a plot in a beautiful cemetery fairly close by. Lauren arranged for the headstone to be inscribed, delivered, and placed. Molly finds a Methodist minister to perform the burial service and advises him of all the particulars. She creates a beautiful flyer that she and Don distribute to local shelters, kitchens, street vendors, churches, and other locations where homeless individuals meet. This is clearly one of the toughest jobs Molly has ever had, but things are falling into place nicely.

In the midst of all these activities, everything stops for a Thanksgiving Day celebration. Don leaves for Rhode

Island on the day before Thanksgiving, and will return on the day after the holiday. Even though it's a fairly short trip, he always rents a car, so he can take Jasper. The weather is cool and can be unpredictable this time of year. He told his mother all about Molly, and she looks forward to the day they can meet--she saw the passion in her son's eyes.

Molly misses Don and Jasper, but has a wonderful Thanksgiving at Alma de Lucy. She doesn't care much for getting up at 5:00 a.m. to help Lucy in the kitchen, however. And it's almost impossible to get Alli up, but she promised to help; reluctantly, she finally gets out of bed. After eating breakfast, the trio gets to work on the wonderful meal Lucy has planned.

Bedecked in glistening white tablecloths and candles, the tables are all set when the women come into the dining room to be seated. Molly comes out of the kitchen and stands at the front of the room. "Welcome, ladies!" Molly says. "Doesn't it smell marvelous in here?" The group responds affirmatively.

"While Lucy and Alli are putting the finishing touches on our dinner, I'd like to say a few words." Molly smiles warmly. "I've always loved Thanksgiving. But until this year, I've never had to focus on the true meaning of the holiday, and what I have to be thankful for." Molly walks between the two tables and continues speaking. "That's all changed since I came here to Alma de Lucy. I'm so thankful I had a place like this to go to when I lost my job and my lodging."

Molly takes a few steps back to make eye contact with the guests on both sides of where she was standing. "If you're like me, some days you may think you don't have much to be thankful for. But, we do have things to be thankful for--we have each other, we have the shelter, we have wonderful meals, we have access to health care at the free clinic, and some programs to assist us. I could go on, but sometimes it seems like the *little things* are what help us the most to feel better."

Molly looks toward the kitchen and doesn't see a signal that the dinner is ready. "By *little things*, I'm talking about people thanking us for acts of kindness, for a door opened, a seat saved, a note from a loved one, etc. Recently, I created a place in my heart where I store memories of these *little things*, and I call it my *Bank of Thanks*. When someone performs a kind act for me, or thanks me for something I did for them, I make a *deposit* in my bank and hold it in my heart. Do I ever make withdrawals? Every time I feel down or like I don't have anything to be thankful for, I make a *withdrawal* of fond memories, I recall them, and I feel better. I just wanted to share this with you, because you may like to try it, too."

Alli signals Molly that dinner will be served in five minutes. "Great! I just got the signal that dinner will be served in five minutes. During that time, I'd like to tell you something I'm thankful for, and then we can go around the table and anyone who wants to can say what she is thankful for." Molly looks down and says, "I give thanks for this wonderful day to share and give thanks freely."

Alli steps out of the kitchen, bows her head and says, "I give thanks for all of my new friends and their incredible support." A few women notice that her eyes have become moist.

Then the next woman says, "I give thanks for my faith that sustains me." With heads bowed, one by one, many of the women give thanks.

Finally there's a lull, but after a few seconds, another woman says in a soft voice, "I give thanks for the wonderful memories I have that help me over the hard bumps."

Molly concludes with, "We thank each one of you for sharing your special thoughts and thankfulness with the rest of us. Now, Lucy will say the blessing, and then we'll all partake of this scrumptious feast she has prepared."

Heads are bowed as Lucy says the blessing, and then platters of turkey and bowls of stuffing, mashed potatoes, gravy, green beans, candied yams, and cranberry relish are placed on the tables. Many guests comment on how wonderful the food looks and smells, as they begin to fill their plates. The group is getting very quiet as everyone begins to eat, but a middle-aged guest named Rosie puts her hand up and says, "I know I'm late, but I have something to be thankful for."

"What's that, Rosie?" Lucy asks.

"Yesterday, I was crossing a street in the crosswalk, when I stubbed my toe and started to fall. Someone close to me grabbed my arm and kept me from falling, and for that I'm thankful."

"That's a good one," one of the guests says.

Wow, that makes twelve out of twenty of our guests who have offered thanks, Molly thinks. *What a positive response. It's good to hear them open up a little.* She smiles as she digs into her candied yams.

As the meal winds down, everyone is stuffed--even Axel, as Molly and several guests have been treating him to tidbits of turkey. Lucy announces that pumpkin and apple pies will be served later in the day--between halftime and nap time--whichever comes first. The women who don't follow sports decide to have a checkers tournament, and some play Monopoly or gin rummy. Most of the guests seem truly thankful and joyous, and Lucy and Molly are pleased. It is a beautiful holiday at Alma de Lucy, where hard times and difficulties seem to be suspended for the day.

Molly feels tired and tells Lucy that she's going to go lie down for a while. She curls up on her bed and thinks about how wonderful this day would have been if Mrs. T were here to share it. Tears silently roll down her cheeks. "Next Monday I have to say my final goodbye to you, Mrs. T, and it makes me feel so sad," Molly says out loud. "However, since this is the day for *giving thanks*," she adds, "I'm truly grateful for the time I did have you in my life to treasure." She feels Axel jump up on the bed and curl up by her legs, and they slowly drift off to sleep.

The day of Mrs. T's service, Molly notes that the weather is beautiful--like Indian summer, with temperatures in the 70s. The day is dry and a little hazy, but glorious colors adorn the trees and bushes. Lauren came down from Ithaca late yesterday and stayed at a hotel. She'll meet Molly and Don at the cemetery thirty minutes before the service, which is set for 10:30 a.m. Molly, Don and Axel are there by 9:30 a.m. to ensure that everything is set up correctly.

Lucy has agreed to take care of the guest book and will obtain as many signatures as she can. Tables with refreshments are set up in a tent on an open area of grass, just inside the entrance gates. Don will oversee this activity and assist the guests. The minister arrives and clarifies some last-minute details with Molly and Lauren. The threesome is not prepared, however, for the large, diverse groups of friends and visitors that begin to arrive. Molly estimates the crowd at more than 100 guests, including Lucy, Max, Rudy, and Alli. *This is incredible!* Molly thinks, as her eyes become watery.

At exactly 10:30 a.m., the minister steps onto a small platform and raises a hand to quiet the crowd. He instructs the crowd about the refreshments to follow the service. Then, in complete stillness, he delivers a blessing for Gladys Mae Teaberry and her family and friends. The minister mentions what a loving, delightful humanitarian Glad was, and the guests are touched to hear this confirmation of what they know so well in their hearts.

Lauren follows the minister's blessing. She looks pale and tired, but is poised as she rises to step on the platform. Looking at everyone, she begins to speak. "Good morning! I'm Lauren Rose Teaberry, and I'd like to thank you for attending the memorial service for my grandmother, Gladys Mae Teaberry. One of the fondest memories I have of *Grandma Glad* was the birthday card she gave me for my first birthday, which my mother saved for me."

Lauren opens the card to read. "This is the message she wrote for me: '*At my age, I never thought I would fall in love again. But every time I see you, I fall in love, and my world is renewed. I'll always bless the day you came into my life. I love you, Lauren Rose,*' *Grandma Glad*." Tears quietly roll down Lauren's cheeks.

She points to herself and continues, "Because of *Grandma Glad*, '*my*' world is renewed and '*I*' can love. I'm truly the one who has been blessed, along with anyone who made her acquaintance. Rest in peace, sweet *Grandma Glad*." Lauren steps down and places a perfect white rose on Glad's gravestone, gracefully turns, and sits down next to Molly.

Next, Molly rises to speak. Obviously fatigued, she still manages a small smile. "I'm Molly Rae Armstrong, and I was homeless when I met Glad. In fact, the first time I met Glad, I accidentally kicked her foot and she chewed me out." Almost everyone present snickers at Molly's remark, appreciating the comedy relief.

Molly continues, "To know Glad was to love her. As a term of endearment, I called her *Mrs. T*, and she quickly became the loving grandmother I never had--without any barriers. Many of us can relate wonderful stories about her numerous acts of kindness and love. Glad was selflessly there for us—not just for love, however. She was always there for guidance, encouragement, support, and wonderfully warm hugs."

Molly clears her throat and continues. "Glad's favorite mantra was '*Go to your heart and lead from there,*' which I repeat several times a day." Molly slowly walks to Glad's grave, places a perfect white rose on the gravestone, and looks up toward heaven. "Grandma Glad, you were a beautiful, gracious, and selfless woman whom I will emulate all my life. We all love you and will never forget you, Glad." Molly returns to her chair and sits down next to Lauren. Axel's carrier is on the grass between Molly's and Don's chairs. Lauren places her hand on top of Molly's.

The minister steps up to bless the grave and offer a benediction. Molly and Lauren stand up, and everyone files by to shake their hands, offer condolences, and bless them. Don is first in line--followed by Lucy, Rudy, Alli, and Max. Don hugs and kisses Molly on the cheek, blesses Lauren, and then walks around them to stand behind Molly. He sees Molly's strengths and vulnerabilities, and is filled with admiration and love for her. She's not afraid to put her heart and soul right out there. The more he learns about this amazing woman who has entered his life, the more he knows he wants to be with her forever. He feels Molly's left hand tapping on the side of his leg, and warmly grasps and holds it.

13

LOOKING FOR JOY

Molly's doesn't have school on the day after Mrs. T's memorial service, and is trying to catch up on her studies before midterm. She still has periods of sadness when she misses Mrs. T, but is slowly adjusting to the loss. However, when Lucy feels Molly's moping too much, she sends her on errands. That's not the case today, though, as Lucy is simply busy with two new intakes and needs Molly's help. "Molly," she asks, "do you have time to go to the market this morning?"

"Sure, Lucy," Molly replies as Lucy hands her a shopping list and some cash. She runs to the sleeping room to get her shoes and sees Alli reading on her bed.

"Alli, I've got to run to the market for Lucy," Molly states. "Come and join me--it's a great day for a walk." Alli wavers, but Molly gives her the *pretty please* look, and Alli gives in. Molly wants to check on how Alli's doing and get to know her better. Of course she wants to encourage and support Alli--Alli's self-esteem is still a little tenuous at times. They sign out at the front door, and they're on their way.

The day is sunny, cool and clear--a perfect autumn day. Molly inquires how Alli's volunteer work is going at St. Anthony's Food Bank.

"I love it, Molly," Alli responds. "It feels so good to be helping others. Two weeks ago, I couldn't even help myself."

"You're growing, Alli. Those *baby steps* you've talked about seem to be taking you in a good direction." Alli smiles at Molly.

They get to the market and begin to shop. While rummaging around the crowded produce section, Molly asks Alli what vocation she's been the most interested in--something she may be passionate about. "That's easy," says Alli. "Hands down, it's cooking, especially baking. I love to alter *good* recipes and try to make them *great*." Molly gives her a curious look, and Alli continues.

"There's a good banana bread recipe that I made great by adding butterscotch liqueur, and instead of almonds in my biscotti, I grate pistachios and add pistachio flavoring."

"Wow, maybe Lucy will let you bake," Molly replies. "Your treats sound so yummy!"

An older woman is picking out apples next to them, hears their conversation, and introduces herself. "Excuse me, ladies. I'm Delores Blain--baker and proprietor of the Perfectly Delicious Bakery and Coffee House." Both Alli's and Molly's ears perk up, and they introduce themselves to Mrs. Blain.

Mrs. Blain explains that she overheard what Alli was saying about enhancing recipes, and she's very interested in her ideas. "Would you be willing to come to my bakery and bake your banana bread? If I like it, I'll feature it and will compensate you."

Alli is dumbfounded, but Molly can see that Alli's interest is being aroused. "It sounds like a great opportunity, Alli," Molly interjects.

"Yes, I'll be happy to bake my banana bread for you, Mrs. Blain," Alli responds.

Mrs. Blain takes out a business card and inquires, "I know this is short notice, but could you come to the shop tomorrow? I have some help coming in tomorrow morning, and I'll have more time to spend with you. If that won't work for you, I'll understand."

"I'm available tomorrow. What time do you want me to arrive?" Alli asks.

"Will 7:00 a.m. work for you?"

"Yes, of course. Thank you, Mrs. Blain," Alli responds.

Mrs. Blain writes the date and time on the back of the card and hands it to Alli. "Good. I'll see you then and will enjoy baking with you, Alli," Mrs. Blain says as she heads for the checkout stand.

Molly and Alli high five each other.

"Could this be serendipity, Alli?" Molly queries and Alli smiles. They finish Lucy's shopping and head back to the shelter. There's a bit of a wind today, and it's carrying the smell of burning leaves.

Reminiscing about London, Alli takes a deep breath and says, "If I close my eyes, I'm home in London."

Alli then clears her throat and casually says to Molly, "There's something I'd like to tell you about, Molly."

"Something spicy?" Molly jokes.

Alli replies with a smile, "Well, not yet, but there's potential."

Molly stops walking, turns to face Alli, and asks, "You've met someone? Now I'm really intrigued. Give me all of the details."

In reply, Alli tells Molly about Corey Lyons, a fellow volunteer at St. Anthony's Food Bank. "He's around the same age, with sandy-colored hair, blue eyes, and a good build," Alli says. Molly observed that Alli's eyes seemed to dance when she described Corey.

Alli's facial expression becomes serious. "Corey is divorced, and his ex-wife has custody of their ten year-old daughter, Elizabeth. I'll have to learn more about that situation."

As an afterthought, Alli adds, "Oh, I forgot to mention that he works evenings as a computer technician."

"You mean that your friend is a geek?" Molly asks.

"Yes, a soft-spoken geek," Alli responds, happily. "He's laid back and analytical, too, which counteracts my reactivity."

"How do you know so much? Are you dating?" Molly inquires.

"One day we met at St. Anthony's while taking a coffee break, and he's shown up for coffee with me ever since," Alli says with a smile.

"We have some nice conversations and we laugh a lot--something that's been missing in my life for a long time," Alli relates. "He's interested in the next step, and wants to take me out for a late lunch some day after we finish our volunteer work. I'm thinking about it."

Molly looks at Alli and says, "I'm not going to give you any advice, Alli--you're a grownup. But I want you to know that I'll support your decision, whatever you decide."

Alli thanks Molly and catches her off guard with a hug. They resume walking to the shelter. Molly feels honored that Alli opened up to her. *It's early for her to start dating, but I hope this turns out well for Alli*, Molly thinks. Then she smiles when she remembers how she met Don, and it becomes apparent that coffee is the culprit.

When they get to the shelter, Alli takes the groceries to the kitchen, and Molly grabs her backpack and goes to her bed to study. She makes a mental note to go to the thrift shop later to look for a chef's coat or nice apron for Alli. After all, if she's going to be a baker, she needs to look the part. *Thank heavens for my unemployment check*, Molly thinks.

Since she doesn't have to pay room and board, she can squeeze out a small perk or two on special occasions.

The next day, Molly is having a quiet morning at the shelter. Thinking about Don is becoming the bright spot of Molly's day. She realizes how lucky she is to have him in her life. He's stuck by her, especially from the time Mrs. T died, through the grieving process, and Mrs. T's memorial service. Molly would like to do something special for him, but doesn't know what yet. He's truly her counterpart, and they complement each other. In fact, they rarely disagree on anything. These are important qualities for a relationship, and chemistry has been there since day one.

Molly decides to take an in-depth look at Don's character, and creates an alphabetical list of his good attributes--from *attentive* to *zippy*. *Well, he zips around on his motorcycle*, she thinks. Looking at the list, Molly decides that his three most outstanding qualities are honesty, compassion, and respect--not to mention the fact that he's outrageously appealing. "I've got to find a way to show him how much I love and appreciate him," Molly says to herself. "I've got money in the bank for a special evening--now all I need is a plan." Mrs. T would say, "Keep looking; it will come to you." *And, so it will*, she tells herself confidently.

Molly's cell phone rings loudly. She sees *A. Lee* on the display and answers. "Hi, Alli! How are things going at the bakery?"

"I just left, and I feel good about how things went. I was a little rusty, but Delores was very helpful. She had everything ready for me, and I baked twelve loaves of my banana bread."

"Then what happened?" Molly asks.

"Well, while the bread cooled, I helped her prepare the filling for some fruit tarts. The bread was cool by the time we finished that, so we got some coffee and took a break. I sliced the banana bread and we tasted it," Alli reports.

"I'll bet it was great. What did Delores say?"

Alli continues in an upbeat tone. "The banana bread was moist--with walnuts and a distinct hint of butterscotch--and a crunchy, kind of caramelized, crust. Delores said that she likes it a lot and it's the best she's ever tasted."

"Great, Alli! How did she leave things?"

"She's going to test market it in the shop this week and give me feedback on the customers' response. She said she'd call me at the end of the week."

"I'll keep all of my fingers crossed for you, Alli. I have a good feeling about this." Molly looks at the time as she hangs up. *Yipes, it's twelve noon already. I'd better get moving,* she thinks.

In the interim, at the Bean Too Long coffee house, an interesting meeting is about to take place between Don and another Lee family member. Rudy walks through the door and is greeted enthusiastically by Jasper.

"Hey, Rudy! Jasper must have been a Brit in a former life," Don says from behind the bar, laughing. Rudy grins and gives Don the *gee, thanks a lot* look.

"I've just started your tea. You like it with cream and sugar, right?" Rudy nods as he takes off his jacket and sits down at a table.

Don finishes making Rudy's tea, fixes himself a latte, and sits down with Rudy. The two customers present have already been served.

"Tell me again how you got Molly's birth date," Don inquires.

Rudy responds, "Well, Lucy and I have been friends for a long time, and I only asked for the month and day Molly was born--not the year. I told her that you want to have a little surprise party for Molly. I also told Lucy that she's at the top of the guest list. So she looked up the date for me--December 6th--and we're lucky it falls on a Saturday this year."

"What a sweet talker you must be," Don replies as he looks out the front window.

Rudy grins, "Want some lessons from the master, my friend? Hey, why do you keep looking out the window?"

"Molly's been known to drop by unexpectedly," Don explains. "She isn't aware that we know each other, right?" he inquires of Rudy.

"Not now, but she will on December 6th," Rudy responds. "Now, what did you want to talk to me about?"

Don asks Rudy, "Didn't you tell me that you have some investigative experience?"

"Well, yes," Rudy answers, "as an investigative reporter. Why do you ask?"

"Did Molly ever tell you about her brother, Jason Armstrong?" Don sips his latte.

"She did mention her brother, but didn't go into much detail."

Don continues, "I want to reunite them for Molly's birthday, and I want you to find Jason."

"Wow, that's a tall order," Rudy says, but Don can see the wheels turning in his head.

"I'll compensate you, of course," Don offers.

"I wouldn't hear of it--Molly's my good friend, and she's helping my sister, Alli," Rudy says. "However, may I bother you for a biscuit to go with my tea?"

"Of course," Don responds, disappearing behind the counter to warm up a blueberry vanilla scone and grab some butter. He serves Rudy, and sits back down.

"Thanks, mate!" Rudy says as he butters his scone. "I'll be happy to search for Jason. Give me any info that you have, and I'll start tomorrow."

Don glances out the front window and says, "Molly alert! She's heading toward the shop."

Rudy quickly wraps the rest of his scone in a napkin and grabs his jacket. "I'll slip out the back. Call me with the details after Molly leaves." He downs another swig of tea and takes off.

Don says, "Thanks, Rudy. I'll call you later," as he gets up and starts to clean the table.

The two customers are leaving when Molly gets to the front door. Don notices that Andrea Bocelli's music is playing on the sound system. When Molly enters the café, Don goes down on one knee, and with arms extended begins to sing a duet in Italian with Bocelli. Molly approaches the kneeling Don, takes his hands and raises him up.

"Ah, my Scaramouch! At last, you've dropped your mask, and your lady is pleased," Molly intones with dramatic flair and a flirty look.

Don flashes a handsome grin as he puts an arm around her waist and pulls her in next to his body. "Aye, I'm unable to kiss you with my mask on." Molly breaks character and starts to laugh. Don pulls her in tighter and gives her a passionate kiss as he slowly releases his grasp.

Molly begins to fan her face, "Whew! Remind me to stop by more often."

They become aware of someone else in the café and turn to see one of the customers who just left. They didn't even hear him come back through the door. The man puts on his hat and says, "I forgot my hat. Good luck with your auditions," as he leaves again.

Don and Molly both crack up. "Do I get the part, Dear?" Molly inquires.

Don grins as he looks at his beautiful girlfriend. "I pray that you'll always be my leading lady," he says, as he places a tender kiss on the tip of her nose. "Now, what may I fix for you?"

"Give me a double shot of whatever you've been drinking--or were you smoking?" Molly chides with a grin. "Then sit down; I want to tell you something. Hey," she wonders, "where's *President* Jasper?"

Don replies, "Can't you hear his snoring? He's in the backroom, napping in his bed."

Thinking it best to ditch the caffeine at this point, Don pours a couple of lemonades, serves Molly, and sits down. "Now, to what do I owe the honor of this gracious visit?"

"I've been thinking about what a wonderful man you are," Molly begins. "You've stayed by my side and supported me through some really tough times, and I want you to know how much I appreciate all that you do."

Don looks touched and replies, "You don't have to thank me, Honey. I'll always be there for you--it's really easy when you genuinely love and care for the other person."

Molly smiles at Don. "I believe it's time I told you how much you mean to me and how much I love you." Don's speechless, as he recalls how he prayed for and envisioned this moment. He's afraid his response will sound like a cliché if he tries to verbalize it, so he just reaches out and holds her hand.

With her other hand, Molly takes out an envelope she was hiding under the table and hands it to Don. He opens a romantic thank-you card in which Molly states that she's going to take him out on a date. "A date?" Don inquires.

"Yes, and it's my treat," Molly responds. "Write DATE on Sunday, December 7, on your calendar. I'm taking you to that new French restaurant *Le Beaux*, for dinner--it's getting great reviews. And then, we're going to a Knicks game."

Don's eyes light up. "What a great present--I'm excited. Who are the Knicks playing?"

"The Chicago Bulls," Molly replies.

"That will be a great game to see. Thanks, Honey!" *I'm sure glad she didn't schedule this on her birthday*, Don thinks.

Molly's cell phone rings, and she has a short conversation. "Sure, Lucy, I'll do that right away," she says and hangs up. She announces that she has to leave, as Lucy asked her to pick up some cleaning supplies on the way home.

"Oh, before I go, I want to tell you that Alli may get a job at a bakery," Molly says. "Alli and I met the proprietor, Delores Blain, in the market, and she's invited Alli to bake with her."

"What bakery?" Don inquires. "I've been thinking about outsourcing the treats and desserts that we serve, and I need to find a local baker."

"But I love your desserts, Honey," Molly says--playfully tousling his hair. "However, if you didn't bake so much, perhaps you'd have more time for us."

Don chuckles. "Is that what the wench wants? Well, I'll call that bakery today and see what I can arrange. There's just one thing," he continues. "I need the name of the bakery."

"Oh, minor details, Captain! I think it's called the Perfectly Delicious Bakery."

"I'll have to look Delores Blain up. I hope things go well for Alli. Keep me posted," Don says. *I'll have to check on birthday cakes, too,* he thinks.

Don and Molly stand up and affectionately kiss good-bye, before Molly takes off. Don truly savors the moment--he's genuinely happy and has never felt this way about any woman. *The great part is that she apparently loves me the way I am,* Don muses. He realizes that it never works when one person tries to make the other into someone he or she's not. "Molly's my counterpart," Don says aloud as he's cleaning tables. "That's why this works so well."

Reality finally sets in, and Don remembers that he told Rudy he would call. He puts the dishes in the sink and takes out his phone. Rudy answers and Don gives him all the information he has about Molly's brother.

"His name is Jason T. Armstrong--I don't know what the T stands for--and he's 13 years old. That would make his birth year 2000 or 2001, depending on the month he was born in."

Rudy replies, "Hold on a second while I write all this down." After a few seconds, he says "OK, go on."

Don continues, "The only other thing I know is that the last foster mother assigned to Jason by CPS is named Alice Gordon. I think she lives in the Bronx. Molly spoke with her, and Alice doesn't know where Jason was reassigned to."

"That's not a lot to go on, but I'll take it from here," Rudy states.

"I really appreciate this, Rudy. Keep me posted," Don requests.

Rudy responds, "OK, mate. I'll talk with you later," and they hang up.

By this time, Molly has picked up the cleaning supplies and is on her way to the shelter. She warmly thinks about Don and smiles. For her, it's just plain scary how right this relationship feels. Suddenly, her dear friend Mrs. T pops into her head and Molly remembers something. *Mrs. T always said, "Go to your heart and lead from there."* Once again, Mrs. T was right.

14

PARTY PREP

Don's working the afternoon shift today, so he's just arriving at the cafe when Rudy calls. "Hi, Rudy," he says. "What's up?"

"Hey, Don!" Rudy replies. "I wanted to let you know that I may have a good lead on Jason's location. Also, I think I know where he goes to school."

"Great! I hope you find him soon--Molly's surprise party is less than two weeks away," Don says. "And, speaking about the party, I'll need your help."

"Sure, Don. What do you need me to do?"

"I'll make plans with Molly, and I will get her to the café around 7:00 p.m.--to supposedly pick up something I forgot," Don explains. "The door will be unlocked because Doug Stanley will be working. Ten or so guests should arrive here by 6:45 p.m.--before Molly and I get here--including you and Jason."

"Let me guess! You want all of us to hide," Rudy adds.

Don answers, "Of course--it's a *surprise* party. Would you please take care of that? But put Jason in the back room with Jasper on his leash. Tell Jason to quiet Jasper and not to come out with him until I tell Molly that you and I have a special birthday gift for her."

"OK, I've got it," Rudy says. "What's for dinner?"

"You're always thinking about your stomach--incessantly. This could very well be an epic event we're planning," Don complains, but without any heat.

After a silent pause, Don continues. "Not to worry--there will be lasagna in the oven."

"Yum," Rudy says. "I'll call you again with any news." They say goodbye and hang up.

The café is empty, so Don uses the time to review his plans for the party. "Let's see, I've got all of the paper goods, a birthday banner, balloons, and drinks," he says aloud. He picks up the menu plan for review--antipasto, lasagna, fresh green salad, cheesy garlic bread, and a triple-layer chocolate birthday cake with vanilla bean ice cream. *What a party this will be*, he thinks. He's left a voice mail message for Molly, and when she calls back, he'll start the ball rolling.

Don's cell phone rings, and he looks at the display. *She's right on cue*, he muses as he answers. "Hi, Honey. How's your day going?"

"Fine, now," Molly responds, and Don grins. "I'm just leaving the library after drafting a paper. What about your day?" she inquires.

"It's been fairly quiet the last hour, so I'm doing paper-work," Don replies. "I got a call from Matthew Ambrose, the CEO of Ambrose and Associates architectural firm."

"Is he someone you've met with for a proposal?" Molly asks.

"Yes, and he's really courting our business. He doesn't have to, though, because I love his work," Don adds.

Molly asks, "What do you mean by *courting our business*?"

Don answers, "Well, he and his wife Michelle want to take us out for dinner at Sakini on Saturday night. I haven't responded because we have our big date on Sunday, and I thought it best to check with you."

"Wow, Sakini is that new Asian fusion restaurant with a reservation list two to three months long. They must really have some pull," Molly says with appreciation. "We're young and can party two nights in a row," she quips.

Don says, "I was hoping you'd say that." He pumps his fist, as Molly has taken the bait. He continues, "I love Asian food. I'll call him back to confirm and get the details."

"Sounds like fun," Molly replies.

"Oops, some customers just came in, so I've got to go, Honey. Love you," Don says.

"Love you too," Molly replies with a lovesick grin. *He's the greatest*, she thinks.

Either on her way to or from school, Molly always visits the site where Mrs. T used to live. Everything's gone now, which makes Molly sad, but she always stops to give Mrs. T a message. Today the message is, "I'm your instrument, Mrs. T. You and I are going to do so much good. I love and miss you." Molly heads for the shelter to finish her paper, and her thoughts turn to Lauren. They connect via phone at least once a week, and Molly's happy that they stay in touch. She feels that a friendship may be developing, which is a relatively new experience for Molly. A funny thought hits Molly, and she chuckles. *Lauren is now becoming Mini T.*

During the next two days, Don orders the food items for the party from his supplier, and decides to order the cake from Delores Blain, the baker Molly told him about. Don accesses Yelp on his laptop, finds the Perfectly Delicious Bakery and Coffee House, and gives the bakery a call. He introduces himself and tells Mrs. Blain that his girlfriend, Molly, told him about her bakery. Delores remembers meeting Molly at the market.

"Molly's going to need a 25th birthday cake for a party on December 6," Don says.

"I'd be happy to bake her birthday cake for the party, if you like." Before Don can tell her what he's thinking about, she immediately tells him her recommendation. "This is my most popular cake," she says. "It has three layers of dark chocolate cake, raspberry cream filling with Chambord Liqueur, and chocolate mocha frosting."

"Perfect!" says Don. "Of course, it has to say *Happy 25th Birthday, Molly*! on top."

"Naturally," Mrs. Blain replies. She adds, "I'll deliver the cake within an hour before the party begins."

"That will help immensely, and bring your invoice," Don says gratefully. "Oh, on another note, I not only own and manage the Bean Too Long Café; I'm also working on my master's degree at the City College of New York. I'm thinking about outsourcing the preparation of our delicious desserts to free up some time. Would you be interested in talking with me about this, Mrs. Blain?" he queries.

"Please, call me Delores," she says. "Yes, I'd like to discuss your ideas. What would be the next step?"

"Well, one good thing is I can taste your product at Molly's party. Please stay at the party and join the fun," Don coaxes. "We can schedule a meeting anytime to discuss my thoughts on outsourcing desserts."

"Thank you for your kind invitation--that sounds very nice. What time would you like me to arrive?"

"No later than 6:45 p.m.--it's a surprise party. Someone will tell you where to hide after you arrive. I'll bring Molly to the café--under false pretenses, of course--around 7:00 p.m."

"It sounds like fun. I'll be there!"

"Oh, bring your appetite, too, Delores. I'll be serving lasagna."

"Wonderful!" Delores responds. "I'll see you on December 6ᵗʰ."

They hang up. *Wow, cake par excellence for my sweetheart,* Don reflects with a smile.

On Friday afternoon, December 5, Rudy calls again. When Don answers the phone, Rudy says excitedly, "I've found where Jason lives. I've been talking with Sandy Rutherford, his foster mother, and we're waiting for Jason to get home from school."

"What great news," as Don pumps his fist in the air enthusiastically. "I knew you could find him."

"Yeah, yeah, I get an extra piece of cake."

"So, how did you find him?" Don inquires.

"You know I never reveal trade secrets," Rudy quips.

"Come on, Rudy. I'm the one who asked you to do this," Don says, sounding perplexed. "Now, how did you find Jason?"

"Well, *theoretically,* of course, let's say that an investigator friend of mine has a sweet love interest who works in the CPS office. Occasionally, she can be persuaded to look up information, with a promise that the source of the data will never be revealed." Rudy takes a swallow of something, and continues. "Now, my investigator friend is smart and knows that the love interest--whom he wants to continue seeing--could lose her job and be prosecuted. So, he tells me that his lips are sealed. That's all I know."

"And I know you can't reveal your source, right?" Don asks.

"Right!" Rudy replies.

"Well, I sure hope your *investigator friend* doesn't suffer any bad consequences."

"He's cool!" Rudy aptly changes the subject. "Hey! I'll let you know later how it goes with Jason."

Before he hangs up, Rudy adds, "Oh, and please include a man named Corey Lyons on the guest list. He's a friend of Alli's."

Don teases Rudy with, "Oh, and I'll invite the mayor and you can invite the queen."

"Unfortunately, her highness is booked. I already asked her," Rudy says without missing a beat.

"Good heavens, we've been snubbed. I'll talk with you later, Rudy." The pieces are coming together nicely, and Don can't wait for the party.

When Saturday arrives, Don is both happy and nervous. He wants Molly's birthday to be the best, and he hopes he can pull it off. Rudy called him back late last night and told him how excited Jason is. Mrs. Rutherford will bring him to the party and will pick him up at 9:00 p.m., when she would like to meet Molly. Rudy also briefed Jason on their plan to surprise Molly by having him come out of the back room on cue, following Jasper's lead.

Most of the party preparations are complete, but Don and Jasper are heading for the shop to take care of some last minute details. Since Molly sometimes stops by unexpectedly, the decorating will definitely have to be done at the last minute, but Rudy said he'll take care of it. They've been telling their patrons for two weeks about the private party, but can't put a sign on the door until after Don and Molly arrive this evening. If Molly saw the sign, she would get inquisitive, and probably be suspicious.

Amy Adler-Smith, one of the part-time baristas, greets Don and Jasper as they walk through the door. She reports that business has been steady, and that Doug Stanley called to say he'll be working the party tonight. Doug is Don's other part-time barista. Don spoke with Doug about the private party last week, and advised him that he can work the party for his regular salary, but may not get any tips. Doug is fine with that--he will get tips on his shift from 2:00 p.m. to 6:30 p.m. Don calls Doug to confirm, checks all the food, drinks, and party supplies, and feels that everything's in order. Doug will put the lasagna in the oven to bake at 6:00 p.m., and Don puts a reminder note on the oven door. He looks at Jasper before they leave and says, "And, don't you give Molly's surprise party away. You hear?" Jasper yelps.

15

THE 25ᵀᴴ SURPRISE

Late in the afternoon, Molly tells Lucy that an architect and his wife are taking her and Don to dinner at Sakini.

"Wow, Molly! That place is hot now, and I hear the tempura is to die for," Lucy says.

"I can't wait," Molly replies. "These people must know someone, because Sakini is booked for months at a time."

"If I'm still awake when you get in tonight, I want to hear all about it," Lucy says--secretly grinning inside.

"OK," Molly says with a smile, "and I better hit the shower because Don's picking me up in an hour." Molly is hiding her own secret little grin because this is going to be a fabulous birthday, and no one knows. *A quarter of a century is quite a milestone,* she thinks on her way to the shower, but she doesn't know if she's emotionally ready for a big celebration of any kind.

Alli passes Molly in the hall. She's dressed nicely and has fixed her hair in a jazzy style.

"Wow, you look great, Alli. What's the occasion?" Molly inquires.

"Corey's taking me out to dinner," says Alli, fidgeting with her sweater. "I'm nervous, of course," she confesses.

"Mrs. T would tell you to relax and just be yourself. I'll be waiting to hear all about it tomorrow. Oh, and before you go," Molly adds, "have you heard back from Mrs. Blain about the job?"

"Not yet, but it's only been a few days. I'll call her or stop by the bakery on Monday to inquire. Thanks for asking, Molly--you'll be the first to know."

"Great--I'm pulling for you. Have a wonderful time this evening," Molly says as she continues toward the shower.

"You too, Molly! Have fun," Alli says as she heads toward the front door. *Whew, I hope I didn't blow it*, Alli thinks.

Molly has resurrected her one and only little black dress, and it's a good thing she grabbed her black pumps when she left the apartment. All she had to buy was some sheer black stockings. After her shower, she applies some makeup and gets dressed. *Where's my finishing touch?* Molly wonders as she goes through her bag. She sighs when she pulls out Mrs. T's silver-toned lion earrings. Molly had them cleaned by a professional jeweler, and they sparkle. The earrings complete her outfit, which is both simple and elegant. Molly looks in the mirror and touches the earrings with both hands. "A part of you will always be with me, Grandma Glad," she says with melancholy.

The front doorbell rings and Molly goes to the door, wondering where Lucy is. When she opens the door, Don is standing there in slacks, a nice shirt, and a blazer. They both say "Wow!" in unison, and then laugh. "You look stunning, Molly," Don says.

"Thanks, Dear. And you look very handsome," Molly replies. Don escorts her to a compact car and opens the door.

"Where did you get the car?" Molly asks.

"I borrowed it from a friend of mine who has a broken right foot. I didn't want you in the sidecar in all of the exhaust and soot when you're all dolled up. Besides, it's starting to get cold out," Don states.

"That's very thoughtful of you--thanks," Molly says.

They share a little kiss before he puts the car in gear and they drive toward the city. After several blocks, Don suddenly turns right and says, "Darn, I forgot Ambrose's proposal and floor plan at the shop. There are a couple of questions I want to ask him."

"Will we be late?" Molly asks.

"It may be close, but I don't think so," Don replies. A few minutes later, Don parks in front of Bean Too Long and opens Molly's door.

"Honey, do you mind helping me? I'll check the back room; if you'll look behind the counter. It's a bunch of papers clipped together," Don tells her.

Molly gets out of the car and says, "Sure, Honey." The shop is empty and Doug is working behind the counter. Don opens the door, and greets Doug as they enter. Molly is astonished to see people stand up from a crouch behind the counter and shout "Surprise, Molly." Rudy and Alli put up a string of colorful balloons and a birthday banner behind the bar. Doug puts a Private Party sign on the front door. Molly is speechless as each guest comes out from behind the counter to greet her. There are Lucy, Jackie and her baby, Lauren, Max, Mrs. Blain, Rudy, Alli, and her friend Corey Lyons.

Molly states, "I'm just stunned--you sure are a bunch of sneaky people. I'll talk to you later, Lucy and Alli," she growls with a smile.

They all laugh as she turns to Don and says, "I can tell you're the ringleader. This took a lot of planning--behind my back." She motions toward the banner and inquires, "How did you know it's my birthday?"

Don responds coyly, "The proverbial little bird told me. But, before we get to the big lasagna dinner and Mrs. Blain's fabulous cake, there's something we need to give you." He looks at Rudy and says, "Rudy, come over here."

Rudy steps over next to Don, and says "What did I do now, mate?" The guests laugh.

Don takes Molly's arm and guides her to his other side. "Rudy has been very instrumental in helping me find the best birthday gift ever." He motions toward the back room and says, "Jasper, bring Molly her present."

Jasper comes through the curtains on his leash. At the end of the leash is a nice-looking, gangly, black boy with glasses and a huge smile who says, "Hi, Sis."

"Jason," Molly gasps, as she goes to him with tears in her eyes. They hug and kiss each other, and her friends applaud. Molly says, "You look great, Jason, and there's so much we have to talk about." Her tears just keep flowing.

Being cautious and protective of Jason, Sandy Rutherford secretly watches from outside the shop. Observing the reunion unfold, especially Molly's emotional reaction, she feels reassured that these people are legitimate. Besides, CPS told her that Jason has an older sister named Molly Armstrong. She goes back to her vehicle to sit and wait until 9:00 p.m., and pulls a blanket and thermos of hot chocolate from the floor behind the front seat. *Now, if I can remember where I put my MP3 player, I'm all set,* she thinks. "Why drive home in all that heavy traffic, just to turn around and come back?" she says to herself.

Don guides Molly and Jason over to a table and seats them so they can visit. Then he announces loudly, "Everyone, go ahead and help yourselves to the drinks over in the corner of the room, or see Doug behind the counter, if you want one of his delicious concoctions. Dinner will be served in a few minutes." Jason volunteers to get drinks for Molly, Don, and himself. Molly stands up and grabs Don for a hug. She whispers in his ear, "You're the best."

Don sets the food on the counter--buffet style--then fixes plates for Molly and Jason, and serves them. Everyone else forms a line and starts dishing up the delicious meal.

"Save room for birthday cake," Don urges. He fixes a plate for himself and asks to join Molly and Jason.

Brimming with happiness, Jason looks at Molly and says, "Your friends are awesome, Sis--especially Don. He's going to take me on my first motorcycle ride."

She looks at Don and says, "Jason is precious cargo. You'd better be extra careful with him on that bike!" His mouth is full of food, so he nods at Molly.

Molly turns back to Jason, "You'll have to hold Jasper on your lap."

"Cool," Jason says, "Jasper's awesome too. Where's your motorcycle?" he asks Don.

"Out in back. Want to see it?" Don inquires. Jason agrees and they head for the back door. This gives Molly time to go to the restroom and check her makeup before visiting with her friends and acquaintances. She especially wants to hold Jackie's baby boy, Levi.

When Molly comes out of the restroom, Alli is waiting in the hall and gives Molly a warm hug. "Happy Birthday, Molly! Being reunited with your brother is the greatest gift."

"This is my best birthday ever," Molly replies. "You're going to introduce me to Corey, right?"

"Of course; we can go right over there. But first, I wanted to tell you that Delores just followed up with me. She apologized for taking so long, but says she's been dreadfully busy."

"Don't keep me in suspense," Molly responds. "What did she say?"

"She said I'm her number one candidate, and to stop by the shop tomorrow and bring my documentation. The bakery is closed on Sunday, and she'll have more time to talk, so I agreed."

"It sounds very promising, Alli. Let me know how things turn out, and good luck," Molly says, as she touches Alli's arm. "Now, I want to meet *the geek*." They both giggle as they walk across the room.

Alli and Molly wind their way through the guests to the other side of the room. Corey is refilling his drink; he looks up and smiles as the ladies approach.

"Corey, this is my friend Molly Rae Armstrong--*the birthday girl*," Alli says.

Molly smiles and extends her right hand to Corey for a handshake as Alli continues, "Molly, this is my friend Corey Lyons--*the geek*."

"Gee thanks, Alli," Corey chides. "Couldn't you at least introduce me as an IT technician the first time around?" The three of them laugh.

Corey turns to Molly. "Happy birthday wishes, Molly. And thank you for all you do for Alli."

"Oh, Alli's the one doing the work--I'm just support staff."

"Don't be modest, Molly," Alli says. "You're amazing."

"Thanks, Alli. Let's change the subject now," Molly requests. "How was your Thanksgiving, Corey?" The three of them begin a discussion of the Thanksgiving holiday.

When Don and Jason come back in, he enlists Jason's help lighting the birthday candles. Everyone gathers around to sing "Happy Birthday," and Delores begins to cut the cake. Don takes ice cream duty and gives the first plate to Molly, along with a kiss. She takes a couple of bites of cake, and says "Oh my God, this is the best cake ever." Everyone applauds, and Delores smiles and takes a bow.

For the next hour, Molly makes sure she introduces Jason to everyone and visits with her guests. She's so happy to see Lauren, Jackie, and Max again, and to meet Alli's friend Corey. Sandy Rutherford shows up at exactly 9:00 p.m. to meet Molly and take Jason home. Sandy is a slightly overweight, 50ish woman who has sandy-colored hair and likes to wear bright red lipstick. Molly is delighted to meet her and invites her to have a piece of cake and a cup of coffee before they leave. She makes arrangements to meet with Sandy the following week to discuss Jason's future, and the three of them exchange phone numbers. Molly gives Jason a big goodbye hug and kiss, as they walk to the door.

After Jason and Sandy leave, other guests begin to leave, too. Molly takes Rudy aside and thanks him for being a super sleuth and finding Jason. "How did you find my brother--after all of my attempts, when I only got the runaround from CPS?" Molly inquires.

"When Jason was transferred to Sandy Rutherford, the data entry clerk made an error and the system no longer linked you to Jason. CPS recently upgraded its system and the error was corrected when archived data was queried and integrated. Sandy called CPS officials recently, and verified that you're Jason's sister."

"Thank heavens! I can't begin to thank you, Rudy. I'm in your debt," Molly says, as her eyes get watery. "This is the best birthday present anyone could have given me."

He accepts a big hug from her, and she tells him, "I'm so glad to have you for a friend."

Not dwelling on emotional issues, Rudy asks Molly, "So what do you think of Alli's new friend Corey?"

"He seems very nice," Molly responds. "Maybe Alli was in the right place at the right time." Rudy nods in agreement and directs a fond look at his sister.

"Come on, Lucy," Rudy says, and takes Lucy's arm. "I'll escort you to your home, ma'am," he says with flair and a smile. *Always a gentleman*, Molly thinks, as a joyful grin appears on her face.

As soon as they're alone, Jasper curls up in the back room and Don gives Molly a tender hug. "I'm so happy you and

Jason have been reunited. He's really a good kid, and he's bright like his sister," Don remarks.

Molly replies, "Thanks, Don. I can't even verbalize how I feel--relieved, excited, and joyful, for starters."

"You have a lot to assimilate over the next few days--you were separated for six years. Thank heavens he's safe and thriving," Don responds.

"You're right, Don. Add *grateful* to my list of feelings," Molly states. "Now, let's talk about this big surprise party."

"Are you upset with me?" Don inquires.

"At first, I was a little unhappy. I didn't tell anyone that it's my birthday because I really didn't know if I was up to a big celebration emotionally," Molly relates.

Don reacts with, "I'm sorry, Molly. I didn't . . ."

Molly puts two fingers on his lips to quiet him. "Let me finish, Honey. This relationship is new, and we're learning about each other. I learned a lot about you tonight."

"Good, bad, or ugly?" Don asks.

"So far, it's all good," Molly says as she puts her arms around his neck. "You're the sweetest, most thoughtful, clever and handsome guy I've ever met. And you're guaranteed to win an Oscar for your performance tonight."

Don laughs heartily. "I called an actor friend of mine and got some tips. I had a problem lying to you, but wanted you to have a perfect night."

"You and Rudy made it perfect," she replies. "I don't know how I'll ever repay you."

Don frowns as though he's thinking hard, and then his face brightens as he gets an idea. "Be my sweetheart forever, and take me out on a date."

"That sounds like a good deal. How about we start tomorrow?" Molly says as they kiss.

After a couple of steamy caresses and kisses, Molly says, "Honey, I'm totally wrung out after this emotional evening. Would you please take me home?"

"Sure, Honey. You look pretty exhausted. I'll get our jackets."

Molly thinks, *that's one thing I love about Don--he's always a gentleman*. He helps her with her jacket, puts his arm around her, calls Jasper, and they all leave.

16

THE DATE

Molly is jolted out of sleep by the ring of her cell phone. Groggily, she looks at the display to see the name *J Armstrong*. She pushes TALK and answers.

"Jason, is that you?"

"Yes, Sis! I couldn't wait any longer to talk with you," Jason replies. "I just wanted to say hi and tell you how happy I am that your friends found me."

Molly sits up in bed and smiles as she and Jason visit. She tells him about going to a Knicks game with Don tonight, and he tells her that Sandy is taking him shopping for new pants because the ones he has are too short.

"You're growing, Jason. I saw you pack away that lasagna last night," Molly says. They both laugh and continue to talk for about ten more minutes. Jason may have the luck of the draw with Sandy as a foster mother. He seems happy and he's growing like any healthy boy. After they say goodbye, Molly is filled with joy as she gets up to make her bed and go to the dining room for breakfast.

♒

Lucy is in the kitchen, rummaging around in a cabinet for some item she needs.

Molly pokes her head in the door. "Just the person I want to see. May I help you find something, Lucy?"

"No, it's here. I just can't get to it," Lucy grumbles, obviously frustrated. "You can come in and dish yourself up some breakfast, however."

Molly grins and says, "Oh, now that you've won an Oscar for Best Actress, you won't help me anymore." Lucy throws a dishtowel in Molly's face, Molly throws it back, and they have a good laugh. Molly inquires whether Lucy will have some time today to discuss a couple of items.

"I need to talk with you, as well, Molly. How about I take a little coffee break right now?" Molly nods, as she dishes up some breakfast. Lucy grabs a couple of mugs, and they sit down in the empty dining room. Molly sips her coffee and begins.

"I know this is premature, but I'd like to talk with you about my replacement. It will probably be four to six months before the apartment renovations are completed. I want you to know that I'll be happy to train whomever you select for assistant manager--either before or after I move--whatever you prefer," Molly says.

Lucy begins, "I know it will be awhile before you move out, but I'll be delighted for you to train the new assistant manager." Lucy gets a cookie and dunks it in her coffee. "I'd prefer that you train your replacement before you move--if you can work it out that way." Molly nods, and Lucy continues.

"Now, there's something else I want you to consider." Molly looks interested. "I'd like you to think about leaving Axel here as the Alma de Lucy mascot."

"This is a surprise, Lucy. I thought you don't especially care for cats."

"I didn't have much experience with cats, but Axel is different. He's like having a child. Some of the women are crazy about him, and I think he's really good for morale," Lucy says.

"I've given this some thought, Lucy. I love the little guy, but if Don and I end up together, I don't know if Axel will get along with Jasper."

"You can visit him as much as you like," Lucy responds. "Maybe Axel has a higher purpose--just like you, Molly. Please consider leaving him here permanently."

"Oh, you're very good at this, Lucy. I'll feel guilty if I say no." Molly sighs. "OK, I'll give you a trial period of one month, to see how he does after I leave."

Lucy is joyful. "Thank you, Molly. He'll be happy here. And, will you take him for his veterinarian appointments?"

"Now you're milking it, Lucy. You're so persuasive; I'll have to put you on the foundation board. Yes, I'll take him for appointments when I'm available. And, I'll talk with Don about being an alternate when I'm not available."

Lucy touches Molly's hand, smiles, and stands up. "Thank you, Molly. You're wonderful!"

"Wow! Thank you, Lucy. Hang on, there's one more thing I want to discuss, and I've saved my best news for last."

Lucy returns to her seat. Molly's excited and eager to share the news. "When the Gladys Mae Teaberry Charitable Foundation is up and running, the first project I want to work on is doing some remodeling here at Alma de Lucy."

Lucy's eyes get wide and she gasps. After a few seconds pause, she leans in, staring fixedly at Molly, and asks, "What are you considering, Molly?"

Molly takes a piece of paper out of the pocket of her bathrobe. "I've made a tentative list, Lucy. See what you think of these items: kitchen remodel with new lighting, cabinets, appliances, and enlarge it, if possible; enclose the back porch and add six more beds and a cat door; add some bookshelves in the dining room, so it can double as a study, meeting, and training room." She hands the list to Lucy, who's speechless.

Finally, Lucy blurts out, "This is unbelievable."

"We'll see what our donors will supply, of course," Molly replies. "In exchange, Alma de Lucy will have to offer self-improvement classes and workshops for the residents. Once the foundation is up and running, we'll work on developing these programs."

"I've been thinking about that for a long time, but I've never had time to develop them," Lucy responds.

Molly continues, "I think it will be great for me to work with someone I know on the first project--while I'm getting my feet wet. Just keep in mind, by the time the foundation is formed, contractors are interviewed and hired, permits are acquired, etc., it may be six or more months before we begin."

"That's more time for me to dream," Lucy replies. "Thank you, Molly. It all sounds wonderful." Lucy's eyes get teary, and Molly hugs her.

Suddenly, there's a loud banging on the front door, and the bell rings. They hear Alli calling their names, and Lucy opens the door. "I got a full-time job at the Perfectly Delicious Bakery," Alli says with excitement, as she dances around the alley in her new pink and black apron that Molly bought for her at the thrift shop.

"That's fantastic!" Molly says, beaming, as she throws her arms around Alli and gives her a big hug.

"Congratulations," adds Lucy. "That's great news--we'll celebrate at dinner tonight."

"I was up front with Delores about my history of drug abuse, too," Alli volunteered.

"What did she say?" Lucy inquires.

"She asked what I'm doing to rehabilitate myself, and I told her about my group meetings, volunteer work, and how wonderfully supportive everyone here is." Alli looks at Lucy and Molly, and continues. "Delores told me that she can't have an impaired worker--one infraction and I'm out."

"Delores is willing to give you a second chance, Alli," Molly says. "What a terrific person she is."

"She seems very compassionate," Lucy adds.

"I know I'm a very lucky person--to get the job, and such a great boss. I admire Delores a lot and won't take her for granted," Alli says with conviction.

Lucy smiles warmly. "We'll all be behind you, Alli."

"It looks like you have a couple of good things going for you right now. Rudy and I both think Corey seems real nice," Molly reports.

"I think so, too," Alli responds. "We've been on two dates and are just taking it slow. He's going to help me with the CPS paperwork to get visitation rights to see Seth."

"That's great, Alli. It's awesome to see you smiling," Molly observes. They walk toward the door, but Alli stops because it isn't 2:00 p.m. yet.

Lucy opens the door and says, "Come on in, Alli. It's cool, so we'll finish talking inside." The three of them go inside and stand in the hall.

Alli continues. "Oh, and later this week, when my thirty days are up here, Delores said there's a vacant room upstairs from the bakery that can be a makeshift bedroom until I get my own place."

"That's super," Molly responds. "What a nice lady!"

"Yes, I'm thankful. I told Delores I need to get a few paychecks under my belt before I can afford an apartment," Alli says. "Then she gave me a check for $50.00 as a commission on the banana bread. She said that the customers loved it and are requesting mini-loaves they can purchase to give as gifts or take home."

"When are you going to bake some of this famous banana bread for us?" Lucy asks.

Alli smiles and coyly replies, "When you buy some butterscotch liqueur. Now if you nice ladies will excuse me, I can't wait to call Corey and Rudy and tell them the good news." She takes out her cell phone as she ambles down the hall.

Wow, what a morning, Molly thinks as she heads for the shower. Then she plans on working on a paper for school. "It seems like there's always a paper to write," Molly says under her breath.

Don's in a great mood this morning, feeling as though things are moving forward with Molly. Jasper is watching him finish cleaning up the shop after last night's party. He finishes just in time to greet a couple of customers as he unlocks the front door. Three more customers come in, and Don's busy for a good hour with steady traffic. When everyone is served, Don takes the opportunity to call Molly to reconfirm the time for their date. He knows that the Knicks game starts at 8:00 p.m., and he's excited about going there in person.

Molly answers, "Hi, Honey!"

"Good morning, Dear," Don responds. "Did you have a good night's sleep?"

"Yes, until Jason called and woke me up."

"I'll bet he couldn't wait to talk to his big sister."

"Something like that," Molly says. Don can practically hear her smiling over the phone as she continues, "and he commented on how happy he is that you and Rudy found him."

"That's nice. He seems like a really nice kid, Molly. Listen, I called to hear your voice, of course, but I also want to confirm the times for tonight."

"OK," Molly replies, "Pick me up around 5:15 p.m. Our dinner reservation at *Le Beaux* is at 6:00 p.m., and we can pretty much wing it from there. How does that sound?"

"Great! This will be so much fun. See you at 5:15 p.m."

"See you then, Honey," Molly responds. "Be safe!" They hang up.

Right at 5:15 p.m., the front doorbell rings at Alma de Lucy. Lucy answers, greets Don, and calls Molly. While they wait, she takes the opportunity to thank Don for the great birthday party he threw for Molly, and they chat. When Molly comes down the hall, she and Don embrace and leave in Don's borrowed car.

"I'm thrilled about our date," Molly says. "I've never been to Madison Square Garden."

"Well, it's a huge place with lots to do. And when I go to a Knicks game, the air seems charged with electricity," Don tells her.

"I know you're a big Knicks fan. Do you think they'll make a comeback this season?" Molly asks.

"I don't know, Molly. One can always hope, but realistically speaking, it is their new coach's first season," Don observes. "But the fans will be behind him, I'm sure."

Molly and Don continue talking until they need to look for the restaurant. Don asks Molly if he can pick up the tab for parking tonight, and she agrees. When they locate *Le Beaux*, he pulls right up to the curb for valet parking. "Nothing's too good for my sweetheart," Don says as he offers his arm to escort Molly into the restaurant.

When they enter *Le Beaux*, they're blown away by the interior design. The walls are painted a light gray and covered with enormous black-and-white photographs of world-famous couples such as Lucille Ball and Desi Arnaz, Clark Gable and Vivian Leigh, and John Lennon and Yoko Ono. Then there are different sizes of red, pink and silver glittery hearts all over the walls. The chairs and booths are upholstered in red leather, with pink table linens, black-and-white checked placemats, and fresh flowers in vases shaped like the Eiffel Tower. Soft lighting and French music create a romantic, European atmosphere.

"Wow," Molly says, "or maybe I should say *tres chic*." The maître d' seats them in a booth.

"I'm with you," Don says. "This place is incredible!" The waiter shows up with water and menus, and introduces himself as Alain. He's dressed in black trousers, a white shirt and has a black beret on his head. Alain reviews and describes the evening specials and inquires about drink orders. Molly requests mineral water with lime, and Don requests the same. The waiter tells Don and Molly he'll return for their orders in a few minutes. Don looks at Molly and asks if he may order for her. She gladly consents, since the menu is written in French.

"OK, Honey, what's your preference tonight--beef, foul or fish?" Don inquires.

"I think I'll go with fish," Molly replies.

Alain returns with a warm, sliced baguette, fresh butter, a large bottle of mineral water, two chilled glasses, and a small bowl with fresh lime pieces. Don orders bouillabaisse for Molly and boeuf bourguignon for himself. Once Alain is gone, they start to talk about the restaurant atmosphere. Don scoots a little closer to Molly so he can hold her hand. They proceed to have a wonderful evening. The food is delicious--with impeccable seasoning. It's one of those extraordinary meals that you wish would never end. They have time, so they top it off with madeleines and coffee.

Molly pays for the dinner in cash, and Don says, "Thank you for the wonderful meal, Molly. What a great treat. I can't tell you how much I've enjoyed having this dinner with you."

"I want to show my appreciation for all you've done for me. You're a special man, and I enjoyed the dinner and your company, as well," Molly replies. "I never tire of talking with you."

Don holds Molly's hand when they walk out to the curb to wait for the car. *This was so meant to be,* he thinks as he opens the car door for her. When he gets in the car, he reaches over and kisses Molly on the cheek and says, "You're so cute! I love you." Molly blushes and thinks, *Just like a little boy with his first crush--I love it!*

When they arrive at the parking lot near Madison Square Garden, Don gets a good spot because they're a little early. They have a bit of a walk to Madison Square Garden, and Molly is in awe of the complex. Don comments, "I came here three years ago to see the Trans-Siberian Orchestra's Christmas concert. It was phenomenal in this venue--I was blown away."

"I like their music, too, but I've never seen them perform," Molly replies.

"We'll have to fix that," Don says as he squeezes her hand. "And you'll find out what 'sensory overload' feels like."

Don buys a couple of root beers, and when they find their seats, he's happy because they're about a third of the way up from the court. He immediately thanks Molly for the great seats, and they sit down to watch both teams practice. Before the game starts and the players are being introduced with spotlights and loud music, Molly discovers that Don was right--the air is electric. At the end of the first half, the Chicago Bulls are up four points. With so many entertaining activities on the court, Molly isn't watching the Jumbotron.

Don nudges Molly, points at the Jumbotron and says, "Look, Molly. It's a Kiss Cam."

Molly looks up to see herself and Don on the Jumbotron. "What do we do?" she asks, excited about being on the big screen for everyone to see.

Don leans over and says, "We kiss." He puts his hands on her face and kisses her warmly while the audience claps and yells. That kiss transcends Molly to another place and she doesn't even hear the raucous fans. Her thoughts are racing to label this new feeling. *I believe I just surrendered, and I'm not scared,* Molly thinks, looking at Don with a wide grin on her face.

The game resumes and is very close. Practically the whole arena goes silent when a player named Carmello appears to be injured, but he finally gets up and shakes it off.

The fans cheer loudly, and Molly says to Don, "I could get addicted to this."

Don smiles and replies, "Umm, I love to create monsters." He and Molly laugh. They're both yelling when the

Knicks win the game with a three point *buzzer beater*, as Don calls it. All of the Knicks fans are charged up as everyone files out to leave.

When Molly and Don get in the car, Don asks, "How would you like to go to the park for a little walk? We've been sitting a lot, and there's supposed to be a harvest moon tonight."

"That sounds really good," Molly replies. Don exits the parking deck and drives toward the park. They discuss the game most of the way.

When Don pulls into the parking lot at the park, Molly comments, "Hey, we're back at Hillcrest Greens."

"Sure, don't you like to return to the scene of the crime?" Don queries.

Molly coyly inquires, "And what crime would that be?"

"When I first grabbed the wench and placed a kiss on her sweet lips," Don replies.

"Well, the wench has issued a warning and is ready to retaliate," Molly comments as she hops out of the car and takes off running toward the fountain. Don runs after her and pulls a coin out of his pocket.

"What are you doing?" Molly questions.

Don turns his back to the fountain and throws the coin over his shoulder into the water. "I wished that the wench won't retaliate, and that she'll see me in a whole new light," Don says. Molly looks at him curiously, as he hands her a coin and invites her to make a wish, which she does. She turns her back, tosses the coin, and turns toward the fountain to make sure her coin went into the water.

Molly turns back around saying "There . . ." to find Don down on one knee in the grass. She gulps, and feels her head reeling. Don's holding a ring box in one hand and takes Molly's hand in the other as he begins to speak.

"From the moment I met you, Molly Rae Armstrong, I knew you were the woman for me. I feel as though I've known you forever. First, I fell for your enchanting personality and sense of humor; then I discovered your intelligence and honesty. I fell for a woman who not only reveals her strengths, but also her vulnerabilities." Don pauses as he opens the ring box to display a gorgeous diamond ring in white gold, and then continues. "Molly, you're my counterpart, and I want to discover all of your wonderful qualities and nuances. Will you please marry me so we can be side by side always as husband and wife?"

Molly has tears running down her cheeks. She is so touched, she can barely speak. Finally, she holds out her left hand and says, "Yes, Don, I'll marry you."

Don slips the beautiful ring on her finger, and rises to kiss Molly passionately. She's still swooning and sits down on the side of the fountain. An image of Mrs. T suddenly pops into Molly's mind and she thinks, *I went to my heart and led from there, and look at the path it's taking me down.* Molly smiles warmly.

"It's your turn, Molly. What did you wish for when you threw your coin in the fountain?" Don asks as he sits down next to her.

Molly turns to look at Don and says, "I wished that Jasper will like his new mother." They laugh so hard, they practically fall into the fountain.

When she and Don stand up to leave *the scene of the crime*, they share one more passionate kiss, with the light of the harvest moon caressing their silhouettes.

THE END

ABOUT THE AUTHOUR

 Susan Kay Gilmore retired as a registered family nurse practitioner in 2008 in order to fully dedicate herself to professional writing.

Now a freelancer, she has published poetry, blogs, nonfiction short stories, and articles for organizations such as Women in Film-LA, Mary's Kitchen in Orange County, as well as *Huntington Harbour Life* magazine. *Molly and Mrs. T* is Gilmore's first book of fiction.

She currently lives with her husband and two cats in Orange County, California.